What My Father

Should Have Told Me

A Novel

Tasha Ray

Alma,
Thanks so much
for your support, it means
the world to me! And thank
you for always being such a pleasure
to play with & be around :) Enjoy!.
xoxo

This is a work of fiction. Names, characters, places, and incidents either are the product of the author's imagination or are used fictitiously. Any resemblance to actual persons, living or dead, events, or locales is entirely coincidental.

Copyright © 2016 by Tasha Ray

ISBN 978-0692736975

ISBN 0692736972

I sought love, ended up with pain, yet gained the

clarity to pen this novel. Thanks for the inspiration.

———————

To my parents and my sister, your love, support,

and encouragement will forever be appreciated.

CHAPTER 1

"I've got to run, but tell the rest of the crew I said bye!" I yell out over my shoulder as I rush off of the plane and into the terminal. "Amber, it was great flying with you again. See you around!" I lied, continuing to speed walk as I breeze past her in the jet way. Truth is, she talked my ear off the entire four hour flight and told so many lies that I was scared we were going to get struck by lightning. I couldn't get off that plane fast enough!

As I continue to hustle my way through the airport, zigzagging through the crowds of people lining up at their gates, I felt the continuous vibration of my cell phone from the inside pocket of my navy blazer.

Without even looking at the caller ID I answer, "Hey Ma, just landed! I'm on my way!"

"Oh, good! I was nervous that your flight was delayed with this weather and that you were going to leave me all alone with your father," she responds in a sarcastic tone.

With a slight chuckle I exclaim, "I wouldn't do that to you, Ma!"

"I'm glad, because you know how much I loathe that man! Just gets on my last nerve sometimes..." going into her usual rant, I cut her off. "I'll see you in few, love you. Bye."

Shaking my head, I hang up and toss the phone into my black Damier print purse that holds my entire life, and continue along the long marble floored terminals of Chicago's O'Hare Airport. All I could think about is why my father had come calling out of the blue like this. I haven't seen or heard from this man in nearly twenty years for God's sake, and now all of a sudden his instinct to be a father has kicked in? It's taking everything in me not to turn around and hop on the next flight back to Washington, D.C. and just go home instead. There may not be much waiting for me when I land, but at least I know it's more than what will be waiting for me tonight at the other end of that dinner table. My disgust for my father isn't something that I've ever aimed to disguise and for as long as I can remember, my mother has shared that same sentiment. I can only imagine the lengths that he had to go to in order to get her to agree to dinner after the way their marriage dissolved.

When I was nine years old, my mother worked the night shift as a nurse at the local hospital and often worked doubles for the overtime pay. She was the ideal image of what a lady and a mother should be; classy and sophisticated with a solid work ethic. She had the best sense of humor, always followed the rules and worked hard, all while putting others before herself. My father on the other hand was more so known for his charm and charisma. With that aside, my father was indeed a very gifted man who taught at one of the most prestigious universities in Illinois. Even though he was extremely intelligent and talented in his own right, if he could take a short cut in life by using his charm and whit, he would. That man could catch the attention of any woman with those faintly grey eyes and pearly white teeth, then mesmerize her with his rehearsed lines and quickly sell her a dream that he would never stick around to fulfill. It was almost as if he used women as his 'studies' and preyed on their weaknesses. When they no longer served a purpose, he discarded of them as if they were disposable and carried on with his life. One would never imagine that someone so well respected amongst his colleagues would be capable of the dirt he perpetuated in his personal life.

Meanwhile, as my mother worked hard earning a living and taking care of me and my brother day in and day out, he was always gone on a "business trip" or at a "speaking engagement" which we later learned was a cover for his numerous affairs. He would act as if he was going out of town for work but instead be on the other side of Chicago in somebody's hotel room, but this is a side we came to know of him later in life as he was always very careful when it came to his mistresses during our younger years. My little brother never even knew of his alternative lifestyle until we were teenagers, but I always had an idea. I always heard the whispers and rumors that circulated, but never wanted to believe them because I loved and respected my father so much growing up. Unbeknownst to us, my father kept up this dual lifestyle for several years. Then one day my mother decided to surprise us and pick me and my brother up from school early, only to come home and walk into her bedroom to find a naked blonde straddling my father in the bed they shared. She was never the same...and neither was I.

She stayed for a while but resented his existence; he stayed too, feeling obligated to somehow erase the images of that day by trying to live up to something he could never be—the husband that she deserved. With each passing day my mother became the very epitome of a bitter woman who was overly suspicious of everything and everyone, often creating scenarios in her own mind that were never really there. Because of the damage my father had caused with his infidelity, I guess it became her reality and she just couldn't see that she had the power to change it by walking away. That was the point that I started to develop resentment for my father and the damage that he single handedly created within our family. The image of him being intimate with another woman in our home was forever ingrained in my mind. No matter what he did to try to recover from that incident, it was too late. The damage was done. The emotional disconnect only grew as I matured and the distance in our bond, which was once so tight, was fading rapidly. Just watching my mother fall apart each day and knowing what caused it lit a fire in me that still burns to this day. That day my father inadvertently showed me that men have the power to tear women down and every day that passed that she stayed, my mother unknowingly reinforced that belief.

Eventually after three years and numerous broken promises, the rumors swirling within the community finally pushed my mother to her breaking point. After trying to move past my father's affairs that never seemed to cease, coupled with all the looks and chatter she endured when she went out in public, she finally packed her bags and moved us out of the city and into the suburbs of Chicago to be near her family. From that point on, my father just sort of faded into the background as nothing more than a distant memory.

I think erasing him from her life completely was the only way for her to cope and rebuild her life, but in doing that, she erased him from our lives too. Even though he wasn't the father I wanted, he's the father I got and for that reason my mother finally convinced me to hear him out after all these years.

Just as I began to make my way through baggage claim towards the airport exit, I hear a familiar voice shouting my name.

"Dulsey! Dulsey!" he continues to shout.

I hesitantly look back out of the corner of my eye to see Tate emerging from a crowd of people, waving his hands in an attempt to get my attention on the other side of the baggage carousel.

"Not today, Satan!" I mutter to myself, cutting my eyes without missing a step in the direction of the nearest taxi stand.

"What the hell is up with this day?" I question myself aloud.

The weather wasn't even on my side. As I exited the airport and headed to hail a taxi, the clouds broke and what was once a light drizzle, suddenly turned into a pounding of torrential rain. The gentleman at the taxi stand quickly pointed me toward an available taxi. With my black mini tote in tow, I toss it in the backseat and hop in, slamming the door behind me. As I catch a glimpse of my curls rapidly turning into a frizzy mess in the driver's rear view mirror, I attempt to catch my breath long enough to direct the driver.

"Ma'am!" The cab driver turns and prepares to ask for directions, instead blurts out, "Wow, you look like you've had a rough day!"

Before I could get myself together and snap back with a witty response, I throw my hands up and respond with what little breath remains, "Yeah, it's been one of those days." I was so disheveled and out of breath from rushing through the airport, that I was positive my outside matched just how disorganized I was feeling on the inside. After getting a second wind, I instruct him to take me to my hotel downtown.

As soon I open the door to my room, I immediately drop my bags, throw the hotel key onto the nightstand, and dive onto the bed. I lay there, frozen in motion for ten minutes trying to pull myself out of this slump and find the energy to make it through the night ahead. Taking a deep breath, I sit up, looking around at this amazing suite. Finally redeeming my hotel points definitely paid off! The view of the city was perfect and just what I needed to calm my thoughts and set my mind at ease.

"A hot shower is all I need right now," trying to give myself a pep talk, I roll out of bed and peel off my navy blue uniform when I hear my phone vibrating against the keys in my purse. Not paying much attention, I hurriedly answer the phone expecting to hear my mom's voice on the other end telling me to hurry up.

"Hey Ma, I'm getting ready! I promise I'll be there on time!"

Just as I was preparing to end the call, I was startled to hear a man's voice instead.

"Hey Dulsey, actually this is Tate! I uhhh, I saw you earlier at the airport and I tried to get your attention, but it looked like you were in a rush."

I pull the phone from my shoulder where it was resting against my cheek as I wrestle through the clothes in my suitcase and press the end call button. I sat back on the bed with the phone in my hand, speechless. I already have to deal with one major disappointment from my past; I don't need him adding any extra drama to what has already been a very long and hectic day. The phone vibrates again. It's Tate calling back. Sighing deeply, I toss the phone back onto the bed and pick up a pen from the nightstand and scribble 'change phone number ASAP' on the notepad as a little reminder. If this wasn't a sign that I've had the same number for too long, I don't know what is.

By this time my nerves are a mess and definitely need some calming. I scramble through the apps on my phone until I find a music streaming app, hoping that some soothing tunes will do the trick. I set my phone on the speaker dock and turn the volume up until I can't hear my own thoughts anymore. With Tamia blaring through the speakers, I finally decide on an outfit for the night. I draped the Givenchy burgundy jumpsuit over the desk chair as I hopped into the shower, still singing every word to Tamia's "Love I'm Yours", off key of course. There's nothing like a good shower sing-a-long session to temporarily take my mind away from all of the day's stressors.

Running nearly fifteen minutes late, I hastily hop out of the black town car in front of the restaurant. I guess my in-shower studio session ran a little long. From several tables away I could already see the aggravation all over my mother's face at my tardiness as the hostess escorts me to their table. I can only imagine what the conversation must've been like as they awaited my arrival.

As I approach the table my mother stands to greet me, "Oh, how nice of you to finally join us, dear!"

I ignore her sarcasm and give her a hug and a kiss on the cheek before I turn my attention to my father who is sitting comfortably in the booth across from us.

"Hey there, baby girl!" he says as he stands up and prepares to hug me.

Coldly, I decline, "I don't need a hug. A simple 'hi' will do for now."

Stunned at the sharpness of my tongue, he sits back down.

"Listen baby girl, I..."

"Clearly you haven't noticed. I'm not a baby anymore," I interject. "I'm 32 if you haven't done the math, but I guess it's easy to lose track of time and birthdays when you've been absent for so long."

"I know. I deserve that and I'm sorry," he hesitates. "I know I have a lot of explaining to do and I know you have years of pent up anger and frustration towards me, but please just give me the opportunity to speak my peace before you just dismiss me."

"Dismiss you?" I couldn't contain my feelings, as I rolled my eyes. "I could never dismiss you! You're the parent, remember? You were the adult in the situation. I never had a choice in whether or not you were going to be present in my life. So just to be clear, I'm only sitting here now solely at my mother's request and not because I came to hear a bunch of excuses that could never fill the 20 year void that you've left in my life."

He looks down as if he was searching for the words to pacify me, but we both know he wouldn't find them. I glance to my right to see my mother staring at me in disbelief.

"Robert," my mother addresses my father, "Can you give us a moment, please?"

He nods in agreement and takes a seat at the bar a few tables over with his back turned slightly towards us.

"Really, Dulsey? This is how you're going to act right now?" she scolds me, shaking her head in disapproval of my actions.

"Ma, I'm the confused one! This man put you through hell and now you're coming to his defense? What's really going on here?"

"Watch your mouth and get that temper in check, honey! If I can sit at this table and hear him out, then so can you! He may not be my husband anymore, but at the end of the day, he is and will always be your father and you will address him with some type of respect!" she pauses her rant, still staring at me while shaking her head, "In here talking to this man like he's somebody off the street!"

"Ma, I apologize. But seeing him after all this time garnered up so many emotions from the past. This situation on top of how hectic this day has been just pushed me over the edge. I honestly don't even think I can do this right now," I explain.

"You're right, maybe you two should just try to talk another time. I know we've both been holding on to some type of resentment all these years, but this is our chance to let that go. I wasn't exactly looking forward to this either, but once we spoke I realized that this is a totally different person sitting in front of me. I don't know what's happened in this man's life to make him go out of his way to find me to reach out to you and your brother, but I would like to at least give him a chance to find out."

At this point my head is throbbing and the only thing I want to see is the exit.

"I understand fully where you're coming from, but I'm just not feeling it today. I'm gonna go."

She agrees, standing up to hug and kiss me good-bye with a look of disdain still lingering in her eyes. As I stand up to leave, my father turns from the bar and makes his way back to the table at my mother's request.

"Is everything okay?" he questions the two of us.

"No. Dulsey isn't feeling well, so maybe you two can reconnect another time. We can stay and finish dinner, but let's just let her go back to her hotel for now."

In total confusion, my father didn't know whether to hug me or shake my hand, so I politely declined either and walked out of the restaurant.

Before I could even make it a few blocks down the road to the hotel, my mother texts, "Honey, IDK where you got this attitude from! I know I didn't raise you to act like this!"

At this very moment I regretted showing her how to text and for even explaining to her what 'IDK' means in the first place. At least if she called like she usually does, I could just ignore it and act like I didn't notice that I missed it and respond later. But now I know she is waiting for an apology for my behavior, so an apology is what she gets...even if I don't truly mean it.

Just as the taxi pulls up to my hotel, I look down at my phone to see Tate calling for the third time. Clearly he can't take the hint that I don't want to talk. With the rain finally subsiding, the sun starts to set in the distance beyond the buildings lining Michigan Avenue. I decide to stroll down the block to clear my head before retreating back up to my room.

CHAPTER 2

I return to my suite after a long walk through downtown and head straight to the wet bar for a bottle of Cabernet Sauvignon. I pull a wine glass from the cabinet just as my cell starts to simultaneously chime and vibrate against the granite counter top of the mini bar. "What now?" I mumble, already annoyed with the day's events.

I flip the switch to the electric fire place and get cozy on the sofa, draping the lilac throw over my legs with a glass of wine and my cell. I unlock my phone to find a text message from Gia.

"Can I ask you a question?" she texts.

I know she's going through some changes within her relationship, so I was almost certain that's what this question is pertaining to. For some reason my friends always come to me for relationship advice, as if I have it all together. I guess that would make me the Dr. Phil of the group.

I respond, "Of course, anything."

She asks, "I know this is a little random, but do you feel in your heart that your soul mate is really out there?"

I can't help but let out a huge sign as I reach for the bottle of wine resting on the side table.

"I think I'm going to need a little more," I say to myself, as I refill my wine glass.

I sit back and think about her question for a few moments before I respond trying to find clarity, especially with all the drama with my father fresh on my mind.

"Yes, I have faith that the yin to my yang exists...and when God feels like the time is right and I've learned all the lessons I need to learn, I'm hopeful that he'll reveal him to me."

"But have you ever felt hopeless? Like, truly hopeless? Because I feel like maybe love isn't meant for me. It's not a feeling of 'I'm never going to find love', but a feeling like 'I'm too damaged for love'," Gia explains.

Feeling a bit emotional, I search for the right words to encourage her to hold onto her faith.

"Of course I've felt hopeless, Gia! You're talking to a woman who hasn't been in a real relationship in years and a woman who has dated damn near half the men on this planet! I've been disappointed a million times, gotten my hopes up a million more and had my heart broken and stomped on, but the thing I have learned from each situation is how I can handle the next one better. I know you remember how low I was a few years ago when I was so depressed and hopeless! I felt stuck and that I would be alone, so I just accepted it. But then I realized that if I didn't want that to be my reality, I needed to make some changes in my life and step outside of my comfort zone. It hasn't been easy, I'm not going to lie, but if you give up now you will be alone." I felt a tear trickling down my cheek as all of my short comings in love flashed through my mind. I had to keep going. "I don't want you to give up, even if that means risking heartbreak to get to the one who will protect your heart. I think above all, I've learned to be patient and to stop making permanent decisions with people whose presence is only temporary in my life."

"Yeah, I just feel like such a mess and giving up is looking like a good option, sadly," she admits.

"Gia, we're all a mess and we're all damaged! You just have to find the person who's not going to do more damage, but be the one who will restore your belief in love which you are so deserving of."

Gia responds, "Yeah. I guess you're right. You are one strong little woman!"

I tease back, "Takes one to know one, Toots!"

Though I typed those words so effortlessly, I wasn't sure if I actually believed them. Lord knows I was just on bended knee in tearful prayer asking the same questions not long ago, so how can I now be the beacon of light and strength for another wounded woman? Just as I was wrestling with this question, I look down to see a call coming in from Josey.

"Hey Josey! You better be telling me you just landed!"

"Girl, you are going to be so mad at me!"

"No, you promised you would come keep me company in Chicago then fly with me back to D.C.! Don't tell me you're flaking on me!"

"I have to, girl! The hubby got hurt in his game earlier, so I had to stay home and play nurse tonight. You know Garrett; over here acting like a big baby, sounding like he's giving birth over a little sprain! Drama!" she says, unable to control her laughter.

"Awww, well I hope he feels better soon. Does that mean you're going to miss our girl's brunch too?"

"Oh, no! I'm there! I am long overdue for a girl's brunch! Plus, I'm sure he'll be better after he gets some rest. He's probably fine now, but you know he likes the attention so he's going to milk this for as long as he can!"

"Of course! I see Garrett hasn't changed one bit. Well, I'll let you get back to your wifely duties and I'll see you soon!"

"Okay, bye!"

I hang up the phone, giggling at the thought of the acting performance Garrett must be putting on for poor Josey. It made me think of my own love life. I glance at the clock and realize it was getting late and I was missing my new love interest's game. "Great. Looks like I'll be solo tonight," griping to myself, surfing through the channels searching for the game.

Preparing to throw myself a pity party and pig out on lots of wine and the greasiest food I could order, I sift through the hotel booklets on the desk in search of the room service menu when I notice the red light flashing on the hotel phone. I've already spoken to everyone who knows I'm in town, so I suspect it may be my father wanting to talk before I jet back to D.C. Shifting my focus, I finally find the room service menu then dial the number for the voicemail on speaker phone as I search for something to fulfill my craving.

"Hey Dee, it's Tate again. I've been trying to reach you on your cell all day. As a last resort, I tried your favorite hotel in the city...and well, it looks like old habits die hard! Fortunately, I remembered this was your favorite place to stay when we used to come to Chicago to visit your family."

Just listening to the sound of his voice message, I feel like I can't down this glass of wine fast enough.

After a slight moment of hesitation he continues, "You know, I really have missed you and I think it would be great if we could see each other and catch up. Anyway, I'm staying at the Ritz, so give me a call if you're up for it."

Suddenly, I was in no mood for room service. I think this bottle of wine will do just fine tonight. I throw the menus onto the kitchen counter and plop back down on the couch as I slide my feet out of my matte black, studded Valentino pumps. All I could do is lay here in utter confusion. Why? Why now? This man walked right out of my life and into the arms of another woman. And now years later he has the audacity to try to waltz back into my world and pick up where he left off like we never skipped a beat?

My mind races as I sprawl my body across the sofa, lost, staring at the ceiling. Sad thing is, even with all the pain that this man has caused me, all I can do is wonder what he wants with me now.

I pick up my cell and scroll through my missed calls. Surely enough, his number is there displayed multiple times highlighted in red.

"I'm sure I'll come to regret this."

I highlight his number and press call...

CHAPTER 3

The phone rings for what seems like an eternity, which in reality turned out to be twice before I hang up and toss my cell back on the counter.

"What am I doing?" I question, angry with myself for giving in to the urge to call.

Just the mere thought of him thrusts me back into the naive, gullible young girl I used to be. I constantly replay our last moments together in my head searching for something that I could never quite put my finger on.

I met Tate almost five years ago while working a flight from Washington D.C. to New York. I'd seen him in the airport on several occasions over the course of a year and even had him on a couple of flights that I was working without ever speaking a word to him. Tate was extremely handsome and charismatic, reminiscent of my father. That's probably what kept me away initially. The ladies would always brag about how much of a gentleman he was and how he was always so well put together. My co-workers, young and old, used to fawn over this man just waiting for any opportunity to flirt. There could be a plane full of people, yet they would always manage to be at his beck and call as if he was the only passenger in business class. It was truly a sight to see and always gave me a good laugh at how silly they looked falling all over him. I remember thinking that could never be me...but the day that all changed started out like any other.

I was called in last minute to fill in for a flight attendant who had gotten sick halfway through what was supposed to be a four day trip. I stepped onto the plane to find out who I would be working the rest of this trip with, when I was greeted by a familiar face. Josey hugged me so tightly and then whispered in my ear, "Thank God they sent you! These old hussies are getting on my nerves! I can't take another throwback Thursday conversation about 'the good ol' days' when they started flying a hundred years ago!"

I could barely contain my laughter at her candor before the other two ladies boarded the plane mid conversation. They briefly introduced themselves after they greeted me simply with a dry "hello" before heading back to the aft of the plane to continue their conversation.

"Dana's okay. She just talks too much for me. But watch out for that Angela chick. She's a piece of work, with her sneaky little self! She's been tap dancing on my last nerve these past two days with all her complaining and nitpicking. Not to mention she's working on husband number three, throwing herself at anything with a pulse," Josey warned, as she eyed her from a distance the entire time.

I threw my bags in the closet and listened to her plan out how we were going to spend our 36 hour layover in Manhattan, before we were abruptly interrupted by the agent letting us know he was ready to start the boarding process. We planned for a little while longer before passengers started to trickle down the jet way. Josey went midway through the cabin to her station for boarding as I greeted everyone that boarded the flight from the front. That's when I saw him. He was standing there looking like he had just stepped out of the pages of GQ with his captivating smile, making it hard to look away. He could've given Brad, Denzel, Will, hell all of them, a run for their money that day. Tate was conversing with what seemed like a fellow business man as they stood in line waiting to board the plane. His charcoal grey pin-striped suit was perfectly tailored, outlining his impressive semi-muscular physique.

Just as he approached the forward galley, before I could even speak, Angela brushed up against my shoulder pushing me back into the galley and out of her way.

"Hello, Mr. Davis! Wonderful to see you again!" she said with the biggest grin on her face, while simultaneously nudging me further into the corner.

Shaking my head at the audacity of my co-worker, he responded, "Nice seeing you again, Angela. You're looking lovely, as usual."

At that point I may have rolled my eyes so hard that they should've gotten stuck, as my mother would say.

"Vultures," I mumbled under my breath as Dana came up to personally greet him as he took his seat. Luckily passengers started to file into the cabin in droves interrupting their conversation, causing them both to head back to the aft of the plane where they were supposed to be working.

It was a very light flight as far as the number of passengers, so business class was practically empty. Upon setting down the chardonnay he requested onto the middle console adjacent to his window seat, the plane jerked for a few moments as we encountered slight turbulence. Tate cupped his hands around mine, slowly guiding the glass down next to him.

"Thank you, I'm so sorry about that!" I apologized and tried to quickly wipe up the few drops that spilled as a result of the bumpy ride. I noticed a spot that spilled onto his pants and handed him a few extra napkins to help soak up the spill.

"Oh, it's fine. There's no need for an apology! A little wine never hurt anybody!"

I nodded and smiled out of embarrassment before attempting to retreat back to the forward galley to hide my face. Before I could escape, I felt a slight tug on my left hand.

Looking over my shoulder I asked, "I'm sorry, did you need something else?"

"You have really got to stop apologizing so much!"

"I know...I'm..." I paused. Trying to catch myself before another "I'm sorry" rolled off my tongue, I glanced over to see that he was amused.

"I haven't seen you on this route before. How long have you been flying?"

"Umm, not too long. It's been almost two years now. I think I've seen you on one of my flights before though. I just usually get stuck working in the back," I explained.

With a look of confusion on his face, he responds, "There's no way I could've overlooked a gem like you. You are absolutely stunning! You've had my full attention from the moment I stepped foot onto this plane."

Oh, he's good! He had me staring into his big brown eyes, listening intently to every eloquent word that slipped from his lips, completely oblivious to everything else around me.

Luckily, Josey came just in time to shift my focus.

"Oh, Lord! Not you too!" she sighed.

"Girl, it's all in his eyes! I'm avoiding eye contact from here on out!" I jokingly explained to no amusement.

"I don't know, Dee. There's just something about him that doesn't sit well with me. I mean, if you want to test the waters, have fun. Just don't get your heart wrapped up in it. I know how you get, you little sap!"

"Josey, please! I don't even think he's interested. I think he's just seeing if he's still got it with the young girls!"

We both giggled as we glanced over at him, sizing him up.

"Then again, he may be a fun ride to ride...don't let me spoil your fun girl," she comments, looking over her shoulder smirking as she walks to the back of the plane.

Just as I finished serving the couple seated in the last row of business class, Tate motioned for another glass of wine. I poured another glass of chardonnay and prepared to replace it with his empty glass, avoid eye contact or conversation, and return to the galley to clean up. Apparently he had other plans.

Before I could walk away after handing him the glass, he gently placed his hand on mine and asked, "Is it okay for you to sit for a moment?"

"Ummm...okay. Maybe for a moment," I responded timidly.

"So how long did you say you've been flying? I really can't believe I've missed the opportunity to speak to you before."

"Just a couple of years. It's not often that someone as junior within the company as I am gets to fly the lead position. I'm pretty shy anyway, so I tend to keep to myself in the back."

"Shy?" he blurted out. "What on earth do you have to be shy about? You are gorgeous! But I'm sure guys tell you that on every flight though, huh?" he questioned.

"Well, not really!" deciding to play along and go the coy route. "It's nice when it happens, but it's not as often as you might think."

"Wow! That's unfortunate."

"And why is that?" I asked.

"Well, simply put, if you were my woman I would remind you everyday of how beautiful you are. I would make sure you never had to question it or wonder. You would know it, so that when you hear it from another man you wouldn't be surprised...or impressed."

"Surprised?" I questioned.

"Yeah. You wouldn't be surprised that someone actually noticed not only your beauty, but noticed you."

He smiled with his perfect white teeth and amazing dimples as he stared squarely into my eyes like he really cared. We spoke for about ten minutes before I noticed Dana and Angela trying to find things to do so that they could get closer and eavesdrop on our conversation. Seizing the moment as a chance to escape the conversation with Tate, I politely excused myself to finish up my duties and tend to the other passengers.

"Damn. I wasn't ready," I mumbled under my breath as I walked to the front.

Walking up behind me, Josey overheard me rambling to myself as I cleaned the galley area.

"Dulsey, what are you talking about?"

"Girl, long story short...he got me."

"What? Who got what, when, huh? I was only gone for 20 minutes, what happened?"

"His charm...his whit...his lips...all of it! But definitely his lips!"

"Oh, no! Dee, I expected more from you!"

"I know! It just felt right, like there was some kind of crazy chemistry that I couldn't deny. He even gave me his business card and asked if he could take me out later on tonight when we get to Manhattan."

"Well, I can say that I've never heard of him giving out his business card to anyone. And girl you know these thirsty heifers have tried! Maybe you're on to something," she stopped then turned back towards me, "but just take your time with this one!"

"I promise!"

"No heart on your sleeve this time, okay?"

"Got it, Josey!"

That night was the first of many that continued for months until it eventually grew into a full-fledged relationship. I was ecstatic! Tate wined and dined me and treated me with the utmost respect. He always made me feel that I really mattered and he would go to any length to show it. Unfortunately, as I later found out, his generosity didn't end with me.

CHAPTER 4

Staring out of the window as the rain drizzles down the autumn leaves brings back a rush of memories. Funny how they say people come into your life for seasons. When Tate left, he took all of the vibrancy of fall with him. Every time I see the leaves change, it reminds me that some people are just as temporary as the weather. Here today, gone tomorrow.

Standing there watching the wind tussle the leaves into the air, my mind drifts back to the day our relationship took a sour turn. I remember thinking that this business trip of his could not have come at a better time. Tate had some meetings in New York and asked if I would accompany him. It wasn't uncommon for me to tag along when he had to take care of business outside of D.C. He would always encourage me to travel out of town with him so that we could explore different cities together. After dating for a year and a half, our relationship became more intense and passionate than anything I had ever experienced. Tate's words far exceeded my expectations and his dedication to his word seemed so real, and at the time I needed that consistency because I hadn't seen that from a man in so long.

It was our first night in the city and we decided to meet up with Josey and her fling of the week for dinner. Josey had slowly become a fan of Tate's once she saw firsthand that he was really invested in our relationship and treated me well. I'm sure it didn't hurt that he would always treat her to dinner whenever we happened to be in the same city at the same time.

After dinner, Tate and I ditched Josey for the night and took the scenic route back to our hotel. The slight fall breeze gently swept the fallen leaves side to side as we cut through Central Park, hand in hand. It truly felt like one of those perfect nights pulled from a movie screen. Strolling down the dimly lit walk way, holding on firmly to each other was the perfect way to end our night. Tate couldn't seem to keep his eyes or his hands off of me which made me feel like a blushing, giddy little girl.

"You look so beautiful tonight." He was staring so intently into my eyes like there was something more that he wanted to say, but just couldn't find the words.

I smiled and glanced away for a moment, and then our eyes met

TASHA RAY

again. "Is everything okay?" I asked Tate out of the blue. I suddenly had an uneasy feeling that just didn't mesh with how well things had been going up until this point.

He smiled and said, "Of course, baby. Why would you ask me that?"

I shook my head and smiled downplaying the moment before replying, "No reason, everything is perfect. I love you."

"I love you, too and I can't wait to get you up to that room to show you how much!"

He pulled me in so close and started to caress the small of my back before grabbing my face and kissing me. The taste of his lips made me forget all of my worries. At that moment, all I wanted was him.

He couldn't swipe the hotel key fast enough with the rate that our passion was overflowing for each other. He burst through the door, pinned me against the wall, then paused suddenly and stared deeply into my eyes without saying a word. I could feel his breath brush across my cheek as his stare lingered. In that moment all the words that I could think of to bring my emotions to life weren't necessary. He already knew. His eyes told me that he already knew of all the heaviness that was on my heart and that he wanted to take it all away and just love me as deeply and as intimately as I would allow. And I let him. No words were spoken that night, only love was made.

The next morning I was awaken by the vibration of his cell phone. I laid there, still too groggy to open my eyes, savoring the last few minutes I had left in bed. I heard Tate's footsteps fade against the tile floors as he took his phone call into the bathroom. I pulled the eggshell colored Egyptian cotton sheets to my shoulders as I sat up to review all the missed calls in my cell.

"Damn! Everybody call at once please," I muttered.

Just as I opened the text from Josey asking how my night went, Tate came out of the bathroom to greet me.

"Morning, baby," he said kissing my cheek before he fell back into bed.

"Good morning!"

I was still all smiles from the night before and couldn't suppress it.

"I have a couple of meetings that I have to tend to this afternoon, so I'm going to be tied up for a few. If you want, I can arrange a spa day for you while I'm out."

This man thinks of everything!

"That would be great. How long are your meetings going to run?"

"Maybe until about four, so that gives you almost five hours to miss me. You okay with that?" he smirked as he tried to put on his sexy face.

"How will I get through five whole hours without that face of yours? Are you kidding me?" I teased back.

I crawled over to him and straddled his hips. "I'm gonna miss you while you're gone," I whispered.

He sat up and kissed me softly on my forehead, then with both hands cradling my cheeks, pulled me down with him as he kissed me gently and began sucking on my bottom lip. Then, once again, his phone started to vibrate out of control.

I pulled away and watched him grab his phone from the night stand and scroll through his messages. Annoyed with all the buzzing and chiming going on with all of his gadgets all morning long, I plopped back over to my side of the bed.

After a few minutes, I grew frustrated. Oblivious to my feelings, he continued to stare at his phone as I slipped into the bathroom for a nice, relaxing shower to calm my nerves. I made sure to close the door loud enough for him to notice my absence and braced myself against the back of the door as soon as it shut.

All I could do is take a deep breath, slipping my black, silk nightgown from my shoulders until it rested against the bathroom floor. Impatient, I turned on the shower and braced the cold water for a few moments waiting for it to finally heat up and warm my body. With my arms crossed grasping my shoulders over my breasts, I closed my eyes allowing my mind to drift. As the hot water trickled down my back, the steam rose creating a thick mist all around me. Then suddenly I felt the warm stroke of Tate's hands glide down my shoulders, pulling me in close to him.

"I'm sorry babe," he said quietly in my ear as he pulled my head back and kissed me lightly. "Looks like we have to cut this trip short. An important client just called and needs to meet with me back home tomorrow morning."

I just stood there without responding. I was so annoyed, but business is business I guess. And with Tate, business always came first. "I know you're upset, but I'll make it up to you when I get back. I'll have my assistant arrange a flight for you after your spa appointments and have a car take you to the airport afterwards."

"You aren't going to fly back with me?" I questioned.

"I can't. Since we're leaving New York early, I'm going to have to move up the meeting I had scheduled for tomorrow and see if I can meet with them tonight over dinner instead. I don't want you sitting around the room, bored all day waiting for me to finish working."

Inhaling deeply before letting out a huge sigh, I turned around and planted my face in his chest. His hands embraced me firmly before they began to journey all over my body. His strong hands grasped the back of my thighs and pulled me up tightly as I wrapped my legs around his waist. Face to face with our foreheads resting against one another, I quietly let out, "I miss you already." Glancing deep into my eyes, he pulled me in tighter then aggressively pressed my back against the shower wall, thrusting himself inside of me.

"You love me?" he whispered.

Barely able to speak, I moan out of pleasure nodding my head yes.

"I wanna hear it...I wanna hear how much you love me," he continued to whisper.

"I love you, baby...more than words..." I attempted to respond.

Paralyzed by the intense passion, I was silent aside from the moans that I couldn't suppress as he continued to thrust himself inside of me, pulling my hair, and whispering in my ear until our bodies quivered uncontrollably in unison. Tate slowly dropped down to his knees, guiding me down until I was resting on the shower floor with my legs still planted around his waist. The water continued to rain down on our glistening bodies as I held him in my arms. We just sat there. There on that shower floor with water splashing in our faces, losing track of time as we talked and stared into each other's eyes.

The funny part is I can't even remember what was said that day, but I'll always remember how he made me feel in that moment — priceless.

Chapter 5

"Damn it, it's almost eleven!" Tate yelled out as he rushed over to the closet where his suit was hanging. "Traffic is going to be a nightmare!"

I sat on the edge of the bed in a plush, white full length robe courtesy of the hotel as I watched him stammer around the room getting dressed piece by piece.

"See you tomorrow, babe. I emailed my assistant earlier about all of the arrangements. She should be sending over the flight info to your phone in a few." He bent over and kissed my forehead gently before darting out the door for his meetings.

Just as the door slammed, his annoying laptop started to chime alerting him of an instant message.

"I told him about the volume on this stupid thing," I blurt out as I walked over to mute his messenger. It wasn't uncommon for him to leave his laptop on. He always wanted to be accessible so that his clients or even his frat brothers could catch up with him when he was in a meeting or unable to take phone calls. I usually never paid it any mind until the first line of that message caught my attention.

"Hey man, ran into your wife this morning! Didn't know you were in NYC. We should link up for lunch and do the double date thing like the old days!"

My mind started to race a million miles a minute trying to make sense of this message. Wife? Really? I had so many questions, but before I jumped to conclusions I figured I would get my own answers. I took a deep breath and sat down in front of the computer, tapping my fingers against the mahogany desk top thinking of the right response to get the clarity that I was desperately seeking. Pretending to be Tate, I responded, "Yeah, I'm in town for a few days. My wife? Where did you run into her?"

He quickly responded, "We're staying at the same hotel! We saw Shelley this morning while we were checking in. She told me she flew in and surprised you while you were here on business, but you were in an early morning meeting. You work too hard man!"

I slammed the laptop shut, sick to my stomach at the thought that I had been involved with a married man for over a year. He never showed any signs. Never wore a ring, had an apartment that I frequently stayed at in Georgetown, I met a lot of his friends, and the only reason I hadn't met his parents is because they passed away several years ago. Or so he said! I fell onto the bed in tears. I was so frustrated and confused that I didn't know where to begin. Then I heard the key enter into the slot of the hotel room door before Tate rushed in shortly after.

"Hey babe, almost forgot my laptop!" as he headed to retrieve it.

"You did, huh?" I questioned him with tears still streaming down my face.

He turned and did a double take before he realized I was upset. Turning to embrace me he asked, "What's wrong? What happened?"

"Your laptop wasn't the only thing you forgot," I responded. He sat there kneeling down in front of me with a puzzled look on his face before I continued. "You forgot to mention that you had a wife. So is that why this trip got cut short all of a sudden? Because she decided to surprise you by coming up here?"

"What? What are you talking about?" Tate stood up and paced the room, shaking his head and angrily glaring at me out of the corner of his eye. "Where did you get this from?" he asked.

"Does it matter?" I prepared to go into interrogation mode. "You don't get to ask the questions at this point. That's my job. So is it true? Have you been married this entire time?"

He stopped pacing; with his back toward me, he glared out of the window in silence.

I stood up out of frustration. "Answer me!" I cried out. He continued to face the window with his back to me making it difficult to communicate or see his facial expressions. The silence between us lingered while my frustration grew as I eagerly waited for his response.

"Would you love me any less if I said yes?" he said in an eerily calm voice, finally breaking the silence.

Staring at him in disbelief, I threw my suitcase onto the bed and shuffled to find anything to throw on. Trying to calm me, Tate attempted to close my suitcase and force me to sit on the bed and talk to him as I pushed him away.

"Don't touch me ever again!" I yelled, warning him as tears continued to swell and trickle down my cheeks.

After continuously trying to console me, he finally withdrew to the side chair in the corner of the room. Watching me closely, his eyes tracked every step I made as I got dressed and gathered my things preparing to leave.

"I love you, Dulsey. I know that may not mean much to you in this moment, but I do. That's all I can say. I just...I...I love you."

I paused for a moment, trying to control my emotions. I hadn't heard those words from a man in so long that I forgot how good it felt. Even if it turned out to be a lie, those words still soothed me in some way. But this time it was different. After the initial moment of euphoria that those words tend to evoke, I was left feeling empty. Things had changed; in that moment, I had changed. I no longer needed the confirmation of this man's love or admiration, no matter how genuine it may have been.

I stood there, lifeless over my suitcase which was packed to capacity as I contemplated my exit strategy. No drama, just a clean getaway without any explanations. No more talking...no more I love you—just good-bye.

He approached me from behind, so close that I could feel his breath tickle the back of my neck. Slowly I turned to face the man whose lies had just shattered the last year and half of my life, realizing it would be our final good-bye. He grabbed me by my arms, pulling me into his body with his eyes closed as if he was trying to prevent tears from falling. Enjoying one last moment in his embrace, I slipped out of his arms and out of the door. As I entered the elevator I could hear the click of the door closing along with that chapter in my life.

As my mom would always quote, "He catches those who think they are wise in their own cleverness, so that their cunning schemes are thwarted." Job 5:13

CHAPTER 6

"Hello?"

"Hey, Dee! It's Tate, don't hang up!" he says quickly. "I'm so glad you finally answered, I was surprised to see you had returned my call! I wasn't sure if I would ever hear your voice again after you hung up in my face earlier."

"Yeah, well, I wasn't sure if you would hear it either. You certainly don't deserve to, so consider this an act of charity."

Tate laughs before responding, "Damn, some things never change, huh? I always did love that smart ass mouth of yours! You always know the right words to say, don't you?"

"No, not always. Right now I could find some for you, but you probably won't like them, so why don't you just tell me why you're calling."

"Ouch! Well, as I'm sure you saw earlier at the airport, I'm in Chicago. I know it may be a shot in the dark, but I was hoping that I would be able to see you after all these years. I know I have a lot of explaining to do, so I just wanted to meet up face to face and talk about everything."

There was an awkward silence as he patiently waits for my response. Lord knows this man has always been my weakness and saying no to him has never come easy.

"It's not me that you've ever had to explain anything to. You should go try that with your wife."

"I see time hasn't softened your blow, but I actually got divorced not long after you walked out on me," he explains.

"Sorry to hear that," I say, unsure of what the proper response should be.

"Ahhh, don't be. It happened. I can thank you in part for it!"

"Thank me? For your divorce?" I question.

"Yeah, but we can talk about that and catch up later if you're up for it."

"Well, what do you have in mind?" I hesitantly respond.

"Your hotel has a great lobby bar, so all you have to do is come downstairs. Maybe we can grab a drink and just talk. Let's say around nine?"

I think for a moment before reluctantly giving in. "I guess I'll see you at nine."

I hang up the phone, staring out of the window reflecting on the bumpy past that Tate and I shared. I felt like I learned to live with an open wound. Every time I sought closure with him before, it seems like he found another way to hurt me whether it be with his words or actions. Continually giving him chances made me feel like I was giving him more bullets to shoot me with because he missed me the first time. It took me going back multiple times to finally get over it, but I never got over the feeling he gave me. I guess deep down I was hoping that time and maturity would change things, and now here I am after all these years hoping for that same thing once again.

———

8:45 pm.

I look down at my phone, anxious for Tate's arrival. At this point I've become a complete ball of nerves, ready to unravel. I decide to go down to the lobby bar a little early to get a drink to calm my nerves. The atmosphere is sensationally elegant and calming. The dim lighting sets the mood, complementing the glamorous crystal chandeliers at the focal points of the perfectly sized seating area. I figured I would grab a drink at the bar before his arrival and then we could make our way to a booth away from prying ears once he arrives.

As I sit at the bar alone, my mind starts to wander. I have been intentionally dodging this man for the past few years hoping that our paths would never cross again, all to avoid this very uneasy feeling that's starting to settle in the pit of my stomach. My adrenaline is pumping just at the thought of seeing his face again, hoping that I would actually be able to say all the things that have weighed heavily on my heart over the years. I'm sure he so freely continued on with his life, but it took me years to truly recover and allow myself to move on after I finally had enough of his misleading words and empty promises. Even still, sadly, he claimed a few of my thoughts from time to time. The power he seems to hold over me after all this time is both baffling and embarrassing to admit. I guess if I was Superman, you could say he's still my kryptonite.

Sensing my anxiety, the bartender approaches me sitting at the secluded end of the bar.

"You look nervous! Can I get you something to take the edge off?"

"Ahhh, yeah! That sounds like a good idea. Ummm, I'll take a vodka soda with a lime," I reply.

"Sure thing," he responds. "So, let me guess..." he continues, catching me off guard, "You're waiting for your blind date! Am I right?"

I nervously laugh before responding, "Not quite! I guess you could say

I'm waiting for someone I used to know."

"Wow! That's deep! Someone you used to know, huh?"

I nod in agreement as he continues to prepare my drink.

"So this 'someone'...is this a person that you would like to get to know again?"

"You know what? I'm not really sure. I guess it depends on which face he decides to show today!" I wittily respond without truly considering his question.

He places a napkin in front of me as he adds the finishing garnishment to my drink. His strong hands and tattoos barely peeking from under his rolled up black sleeves caught my eye as he sets my drink down. I glance up to see him staring at me with a smile before looking for a way to continue the conversation.

"Oh, I'm Kenny by the way," he states, reaching out his hand.

"Nice to meet you Kenny, I'm Dulsey," I brazenly respond. I reach out to shake his hand and he kisses it instead.

"That's a great name!" he responds as I pull my hand back.

"Thanks, I got it from my momma!" I jokingly reply. We both giggle as I take a sip of my drink.

"Not to be too forward, but if this 'someone' turns out to be a person you don't want to get to know again...promise me that you'll come by and tell me how things turn out, because if given the opportunity, you won't regret getting to know me. I tend to get things right the first time."

I nod, smiling to myself at how bold he is while continuing to sip my drink as he walks away to tend to the other guests. That height, those muscles, and his tattoos almost had me forgetting that I already had a man. Well, sort of. But it can't hurt to look, right? Or so I justified it to myself.

Thankfully, the forwardness of the bartender kept my attention off of Tate and the fact that it's after nine and he still hasn't arrived or called. Then again, punctuality and communication were never his strong points, so I guess some things haven't changed with him either.

After two and a half vodka sodas and a few more flirtatious exchanges with the bartender, I look down at my phone and realize that ten thirty is fast approaching and I've yet to hear anything from Tate. Before I could dial his number and give him a piece of my mind, an unfamiliar phone number with a local area code pops up on my cell. Sure that it's Tate calling from another phone, I quickly answer to hear what excuse he has this time.

"You know, showing up over an hour late isn't how I saw this night starting off," I yell into the phone.

"Hey Dulsey, I'm sorry for calling so late but this is actually your father. Your mother gave me your number. I hope you're not upset."

Not expecting to hear his voice on the other end of the phone, I pull the phone away from my ear for a moment as I take a deep breath and redirect my train of thought.

"Ummm...Hey, Robert," struggling for a moment to find the right words, I continue, "I've had a couple drinks, so I'm probably too numb to be upset at this point."

"Is everything okay? Sounds like you were expecting someone else," he questions.

"Just a little man trouble, but that's the story of my life."

"Oh, okay. I understand. Are u still at your hotel up the street from the restaurant?"

"Yep, at the bar downstairs waiting for someone who clearly is never coming."

"Well if you don't mind, I'd like to come see you just for a little bit before I head home and out of the city. Would that be okay?" Before I could respond, he continues, "I promise it will only be for a moment. I hate to leave things on such a sour note before you fly out."

I let out a huge sigh looking around, hoping to see Tate's face. Of course he's nowhere to be found. Letting down my guard I respond, "Why not? Looks like I've been stood up anyway."

"Great! I'll be seeing you in a few then!" he responds, sounding overjoyed.

Fifteen minutes later my father enters, pulls out the chair next to me and sits down at the bar. I signal for Kenny to return to take my father's order as a stalling tactic. I hope he breaks the ice, because I don't want this conversation to go into a downward spiral as it did earlier.

"Hey baby gi...I mean, Dulsey," he quickly corrects himself.

"Hi Robert," I respond, unable to look him in his eyes.

"Well, your mom and I had a great conversation at the restaurant. I think we were able to really bury the hatchet and try to move forward as best we can." Still unable to make eye contact with him, he continues, "I was hoping that we could attempt to do the same thing. I know I have been an absentee father for most of your life, and that's something I will regret forever. You and your brother were my pride and joy. I'm just so thankful for how you guys turned out and the people you've grown up to be." He pauses for a moment, hesitating, "I...I just wish I could say I had something to do with it."

"Well, Robert, I think you did." I finally lift my head and our eyes meet. "Because of you, I've spent the majority of my adult years trying to figure out what love looks like from a man. And for that, I can thank you."

"Listen Dulsey, I didn't come here to anger you or try to make excuses for my poor decisions, but I was hoping that we could at least put it all on the table. I'm willing to hear you out...I mean, that's the least I can do! I know you're frustrated! I know you're angry! I'm not trying to take your right to feel all of those things away from you. All I ask is that once we lay everything out on the table and we talk through this, that you give me an opportunity to be the best father to you possible from this point on. I know I can't make up for the time we lost, I just don't want to lose any more time with you."

Kenny places a glass of whiskey on ice in front of my father, prompting him to pause in mid thought giving me a chance to respond.

"I think I'm willing to hear you out, plus I have a few questions of my own that I need answered."

"Okay. Sounds fair! How about we take this conversation over to the corner booth since the bar is starting to fill up," he suggests.

I nod and follow him away from the small crowd that was slowly pouring into the bar area.

As we walked back to the booth, I thought back to the last time I saw my father almost 20 years ago at my twelfth birthday party. He showed up late with no gift and alcohol on his breath. Not exactly the reason why I wanted that day to be memorable, but that image of my father forever stuck with me. For years I blamed him and his absence for how terrible my dating life had been. I felt like he was a major factor in why I kept choosing losers and allowing men to sell me dreams that I knew deep down would never came to fruition. I used to chase after men thinking that I had to prove to them that I was worthy before it finally dawned on me that I was the prize all along. All those seemingly common sense lessons and daddy advice never made it to my ears, so I had to learn the hard way by giving my love away freely, each time bearing a piece of my soul and feeling all used up by the time I hit 30.

"So where do we begin?" I ask.

"Can I ask you who you were expecting before I came?"

"Just one of my many bad judgment calls in life...a man named Tate."

"So this Tate character, you mind if I ask the back-story?"

"He did what you all do. Cheat, lie, then made me feel like I was crazy for leaving when I called him out on his shit. And then after he calls out of nowhere several years after breaking my heart, I fell for his empty words again and agreed to hear him out one last time...hoping that I would get closure, instead of wondering in the back of my mind 'what if' when it comes to us." Feeling myself start to get emotional, I pause for a moment. "He does this to me every time...and every time I let him," I mumble hanging my head low.

"Baby girl, I know I've missed out on a lot, and I wish I had been able to have these types of conversations with you earlier in life. But you can never allow a man to tell you or show you that he doesn't want you over and over again. One time should be all it takes. All those things that men say like, 'I'm not ready' or making excuses for having other women on the side, really just means that they don't want you, as harsh as it may sound. Now I know that may not be what you want to hear, but coming from a man, that's exactly what he means. So it's up to you to either take that man at his word or be a willing victim of his actions. It may be over, but that's okay! It opens the door for someone better!"

Just as he stops, he lifts my chin up and stares me directly in the eyes. "Look at me Dulsey. Stop wondering if you're good enough because he's not available to you. Don't allow yourself to become a convenience for him again. You've grown into such an amazing woman! You deserve a man who knows that you are too good to pass up and that he would be a fool to give another man the opportunity to do the things that he should be doing for you. And trust me, when you have the right man, he won't hesitate to do the right thing for you."

"You know Robert, this is baffling to me. I hear you...I really do! But if you're so insightful, why couldn't you be all those things for mom? Since you have this incredible sense of clarity, why couldn't you see that you had responsibilities when you had us? Didn't we matter to you? Was I...were we...were we not enough to make you want to be the model of what a man should be instead of trying to undo the damage that your poor choices have had on our lives?"

"Dulsey!" he attempts to defend himself.

"No!" I interject as he tries to cut me off, "Didn't I deserve someone to tell me that I'm worth it and that I'm beautiful and actually mean it? I mean, damn!" I smack the table out of frustration as the tears begin to roll down my face with my head dropping into my hands. I didn't realize how deep my pain and resentment was until this very moment when all of my emotions surfaced at once.

Rubbing my back, trying to console me he suggests, "Well, maybe I should've started by telling you what happened with me all those years ago so maybe you can understand me a little better." I shrug in agreement trying to wipe my tears away.

"After your mother left me and took you guys, I'm not going to lie, I continued to live wrong and selfishly. Your mother and I were so young when we had you and got married. We were literally in high school one day stressing over calculus, then being hit with the real world, raising a small child and struggling to provide, the next. Now,

I'm not making any excuses for my actions, I just want you to understand that I was young and immature. After all, we were kids trying to be adults! But eventually we hit a rough patch in our marriage and instead of talking things out with your mother, I chose to confide in a woman that I was working with at the time. That one affair opened the door to a string of others and created an even greater distance between Sharon and myself. Sharon thought that moving our family to a new town and getting a fresh start would help, and well it did for a while, but the damage had already been done. Your mother was so paranoid and cold towards me, so much so, I couldn't realize why she even wanted to stay. But it never dawned on me until years later that she, being the mature woman that she is, was willing to sacrifice her own happiness so that you and your brother could grow up with both of us. I'm so glad that she eventually decided to leave and find happiness for herself though. That was just something I wasn't willing or able to give any woman for years, simply because I was so consumed with myself. All I wanted to do was drink, have a good time, and make up for what I thought I had missed out on after being married with kids throughout my entire twenties. I went through a phase where I ran from my problems and avoided my responsibilities instead of standing up and facing them like a man. Problem is I wasn't yet a man. All of my bad decisions lead to two additional children out of wedlock by two different women. By the time my forties rolled around, I was stuck trying to put the pieces of my life back together again. My partying ways and drinking habit caused me to lose my job as a professor, and it was difficult to find work at any of the prestigious universities that once celebrated my accolades. I eventually took a position at a local community college and had to work my way back to the top and put each aspect of my life back together."

Completely overwhelmed by what I was hearing, I sat there in silence.

"Dulsey, I know this is a lot for you to digest, but I truly want to be there for you. I know I've missed the chance to give you advice and help guide you in life and love all those years ago, but I'd like that chance now if you'll let me. I just want to be here for you. I don't want to miss another minute!"

Taking a deep breath, I respond, "I know. And maybe we'll get there one day. I think I just need some time to process things."

"I respect that and I understand. I'll give you all the space and time you need. Whenever you need me, just call me since you have my number now," he says with a smile.

"I do, don't I? So that means there's no getting away from me this time!" I joke in an attempt to lighten the mood.

"You couldn't run me off with a shotgun, sweetheart! You're stuck with me this time!"

We shared a laugh before exiting towards the main lobby, and I put my ego aside allowing Robert to give me a huge bear hug before leaving. Turns out I needed it more than he did.

CHAPTER 7

After an emotional night of being stood up and an even more emotionally draining conversation with my father, I was more than ready to head back up to my room and get some rest. After waiting a few moments for the elevator to arrive, I step in and press the 30th floor button. As the doors start to close I hear a man yelling to hold the elevator. I place my arm in between the doors, prompting them to reopen before I realize that it's Tate approaching the elevator. I quickly pull my arm back and push the button to close the elevator doors, but he stumbles on just in time.

Slightly out of breath from his brief sprint, he begins to question me, "Who was that you were just talking to?"

Staring in the opposite direction of him, I remain silent ignoring his existence.

"You're not going to answer me? So you like 'em old now, huh? Retirement age?" he continues.

"Really, now you want to be funny and insulting? How about an 'I'm sorry for being two hours late and standing you up' asshole," I shout out of pure frustration.

He took a moment to calm down and compose himself before continuing, "Look, I'm sorry. A meeting ran long."

"Oh, yeah! You and your meetings! I know all about those 'meetings'," mocking him with air quotes. "I'm sure they did run long!"

"Seriously, Dee! I'm sorry. Let me make this right!" he pleads.

"Tate, you had your chance two hours ago when my tolerance for BS was much higher. I'm afraid your window of opportunity has closed for good, so why don't you just go back to your hotel."

"Dee, just hear me out! I'm in town buying a house for my mom. There were a few unexpected things that came up at the closing, so it ended up pushing the business meeting I had scheduled afterwards back, causing things to run longer than I anticipated. I'm only in town for a couple days, so I had to take care of my business matters first!"

"Yep, it's always about business with you, but at some point you could've had enough respect for me and my time to at least send me a text and let me know. You don't just leave someone hanging for two hours then expect to just show up and everything is peachy!"

"I understand that, and you're right. I jetted over here right after my meeting, but then I saw you having drinks with this guy, so I decided to wait on the other end of the lobby until you were done so we could talk."

Unfazed, I roll my eyes at his weak excuse. Thankfully, I glance up to see the elevator approaching my floor.

"I've explained myself and apologized, so are you going to tell me who grandpa was or what? Are you dating that guy?"

"No."

"So who is he?" Tate continues to press the issue as the elevator reaches my floor.

I pause as the doors open before calmly replying, "My father."

"Come on Dee, that's not funny!" he says, following me off of the elevator.

"Do you think this is a topic I would joke about?"

Finally catching on to how serious I am he responds, "The same father you haven't seen since you were, what, eleven or twelve?"

"One in the same."

Before reaching my room, I quickly turn around and put my hand out stopping Tate in his tracks.

"And where are you going?" I question with my hand still extended.

"I just thought we could finish this conversation."

"Nice try, but as I told you before, that chance has come and gone. This conversation is over. Goodnight."

I continue towards my room and slide the key card in the door, preparing to walk in as my phone rings. I push the door open and notice that it's Jay calling, so I quickly answer.

"Hey babe!"

As I turn to close the door, Tate is standing in the doorway with his foot jammed against it making it impossible to close.

"Hey babe, hold on one moment," I quickly blurt out into the phone before fumbling to place in on mute and head towards Tate.

"Tate, move! I don't feel like doing this with you tonight!" I yell.

"Dee, just give me ten minutes! Just ten! Then you can be done with me forever if that's what you want."

Sighing loudly, I knew he wouldn't leave so I motioned him into the living room area before resuming my call with Jay in the bedroom, noticing that I had accidentally unmuted the phone.

"Sorry about that!" I apologize, hoping he wouldn't ask any questions about the commotion he may have heard in the background. "How was your game?" I ask, quickly changing the subject.

"Oh, it was great! We won, so it looks like we're play-off bound with this one under our belt. How did everything go with your dad earlier?"

"Oh my goodness, Jay. That's such a loaded question! I have so much to tell you, I'm just too exhausted right now. I was actually headed to bed, so can we talk about it tomorrow when I get back?"

"Of course, baby! Get some rest!"

"Ok, I will. Goodnight," I say, hanging up the phone and placing it on the nightstand.

Tate's stoic stance startles me as I turn around. Clearly he has been standing there in the doorway of the bedroom, listening in on my conversation the entire time. Annoyed with his presence and his rudeness, I attempt to ask him to leave but he cuts me off before I can barely get the words out.

"Looks like someone's gotten good at lying themselves over the years...or were you doing that all along?"

"There goes that active imagination of yours! And I didn't lie. I actually do plan on going to bed right now, so this would be a great time for you to leave," as I motion him towards the exit.

"Now we both know you don't want me to do that."

He slowly begins to walk towards me, forcing me to walk backwards until my back is flush against the bedroom wall. Tate is standing in front of me, so close that I could feel the warmth of his breath. Uncomfortable and trying to avoid eye contact, he touches me, immediately taking me back to all those amazingly passionate nights we shared. Every touch sends chills down my body, making me vulnerable to his attempts to seduce me. He pulls my face towards his attempting to kiss me, which pulled me out of my temporary trance. Disappointed with myself, I immediately cringe and push him away. "Okay, this isn't why I agreed to meet up with you. Let me make this clear. You and me? We're done. I've moved on and I'm sure you still have your situation going on, so what are we really doing? Huh? What's the point of it all?"

"You know, that little letter you left that day in New York at the front desk for my wife telling her about our relationship was the last nail in the coffin for us. Even when you and I did the back and forth, you knew it was over between me and Shelley. I only ever wanted you, which is why I finally got that divorce."

Caught off guard, I turn away and peer out of the window. I never thought I would see the day that he would actually make good on his promise to get a divorce. But knowing him, he probably had no choice in the matter. "Well, great. Congratulations. Smart woman. What exactly do you expect me to say?" I ask.

"I don't know, I guess I was just hoping that we could rekindle what we had."

"What we had? You mean a lie? No, thanks. I may have been young and naive then, but I know better now. Going out to expensive restaurants and fucking a married man in fancy hotel rooms isn't my idea of romance and it's not a part of my life that I'm proud of or want to relive."

"Damn, I'm sorry Dee! I didn't know you still felt this way after all this time, especially now that I'm divorced!" he says, stunned by my reaction.

"Just be honest for once, Tate! Had I not left that note for your wife, you'd be up to the same dirty dog antics with a newer, younger version of me. And yeah, I can admit that you broke me back then because I made the mistake of making you my world. I'm not that girl anymore! I don't give men that kind of power! So as far as I'm concerned, the only thing you can do for me at this point in my life is forget you ever knew me."

Tate stood there quiet for a moment at a loss for words.

"Goodnight, Tate."

He throws up his hands, "I guess...goodnight to you, too."

He slowly walks towards the door to exit, then turns back, "I'm really sorry, Dee. I really am."

The door closes, and he's finally on the other side of it. Breathing a sigh of relief, I fall into bed so ready for this day to end.

CHAPTER 8

"Last boarding call for all ticketed passengers on flight 2941 with service to Washington, D.C.," blares through the terminal just as I approach the gate.

Apparently I should've slowed down on the drinks a little earlier. Maybe then I wouldn't have slept through my alarm, causing me to rush nonstop to the airport. Luckily, I boarded the flight just in time and was able to snag a window seat and allow myself to get lost in the view.

It was still early as the sun crept out of the clouds and into plain view. As the plane emerges out of the clouds, I admire the illumination of the city with its lights perfectly lining the streets. As Chicago becomes distant in view, my eyes fixate on the morning dew on my window. It reminded me of all of the tears shed on this very brief trip, but I finally feel like I have been provided with a small bit of closure that I've sought for longer than I can remember. Finding a workable space with my father has given me hope that we can at least be cordial and that I don't have to hold on to all that hate and hurt any longer. Lord knows it has definitely been weighing me down over the years, and closing the door on the Tate saga has given me reassurance that I'm making the right decision by moving forward in my current relationship, instead of being fixated on my past.

Just the thought of Jay has me smiling cheek to cheek. It's amazing how just the thought of someone can excite you and make you forget about anything else. He has been a breath of fresh air for me even though our relationship is still very new. Hell, I'm not even sure if we can consider it a relationship quite yet, but we are definitely on that track and I can't wait to spill the beans to my girls over brunch.

The girls and I made it a point get together as often as possible, no matter where our lives may take us. We've done a pretty good job of sticking to that promise too, up until last year when life threw some unexpected obstacles our way. We decided that brunch in D.C. would be a great way to get back on track, so I decided to cut my Chicago trip a little short to make sure I could be present.

We all met years ago in a flight attendant training class where we hit it off instantly. From there we all moved to the District of Columbia together and became roommates. Taylor was the outspoken one and the first to ditch us when she got engaged and decided to pursue law school. Unfortunately, two months before her wedding, her fiancé died in a car accident. A couple months later she found out that she was pregnant with a baby boy that she now raises alone. Gia was the hopeless romantic of the group. She was ready to be settled down since the day we met and was looking to put anybody in that role whether they were ready or not. She met her on again, off again boyfriend on a flight from JFK to Miami. Being the spontaneous person she is, only a few months after meeting him she decided to follow him to Miami to settle down. Their relationship was so unstable, so she frequently moved back and forth between the two cities before she finally got fed up with his cheating and moved back up north for good. But this time she came back with a toddler, an attitude, and still no ring. Then there's Josephine, but we all call her Josey for short. She was the one who stuck it out with me at work the longest before meeting her baller boo, giving up her man-eating ways, and moving across the country.

And lastly, there's me. Dulsey or Dee, as my close friends call me. I'm the glue that keeps the girls together, always offering up advice when it's needed and the first one they call when something is wrong. Now, I definitely have my own set of issues and I can admit that I haven't been the best judge of character when it comes to men, but I was fortunate to have three of the best women I've ever met to call friends and help me out along the way in return. They were there by my side through the highest of highs and the lowest lows — and I'm talking low! We've been each other's rock through this whole dating debacle and ten years later we're still trying to keep each other on the straight and narrow; especially when it comes to these boys! So as you can imagine, between the four of us we have enough drama in our lives to put reality television out of business.

————-

As soon as the plane lands, a text message comes through from Josey asking me to meet her a little early at The Beacon. I thought it was a little odd being that we were set to meet the rest of the girls there a little before noon, but I figure it must be important, so I oblige her request.

After spending forty-five minutes of my life stuck on I-395 in traffic, I finally make it home. Walking into my brownstone, I feel such a sense of relief coupled with pure happiness to be back in my own space. Between traveling for work and spending time with Jay, I haven't seen a whole lot of this place the past few weeks. Setting my things down in my bedroom, I realize that it's already nine thirty, leaving me an hour to get ready and make it over for brunch to meet Josey. The past few months she's been unusually secretive and has isolated herself from the group, which left me feeling like there was something going on within her relationship but that she wasn't quite ready to talk about it. She's always been the strong one in the bunch; the one who never got attached emotionally when it came to men, so you can imagine our surprise when she was the first one to jump the broom.

I'll never forget how that conversation went a few years ago when she dropped the bomb on us girls at one of our many pow wows. She rushed straight in the door that night, so excited, unable to contain her happiness.

———

"So, girls, guess what?" without taking a breath, she continued before we could get a word in edgewise, "Okay, okay, okay! I'll just tell you! I'm moving!"

"What, where?" we all responded in unison out of confusion.

"To California! Garrett asked me to move in with him!" Josey explained.

"Oh. Okay," Taylor reacted, clearly not in support of her decision.

In an attempt to deflect attention away from Taylor, Gia asked, "So does that mean you guys are getting married? You know, did a proposal come with this arrangement or are you just going to play house?"

Attempt failed. I gave the two of them the hardest side eye, waiting to hear how Josey would respond.

"I mean, probably. One day..." she hesitated, "We...we haven't really gotten that far with the whole marriage thing."

Taylor continued to dig, "I'm confused. Then what exactly is in this for you? What, a few months of free rent? A few bags...some expensive shoes?"

"Maybe! Why? You jealous?" Josey snapped back.

"Well then, enjoy that shit while it lasts because you know how it goes with these famous types. Especially, athletes! You'll be here today and gone tomorrow and we're the ones that are going to have to help you put the pieces of your life back together while he sails off into the sunset with the next chick he pulled off of social media," Taylor explained.

"Really, Taylor? It's funny because I don't recall you having any of these concerns when y'all were sitting court side or enjoy expensive dinners courtesy of Garrett! So he's cool as long as you're benefiting from him, right? He was good enough before today, but now you're worried?" Josey replied, infuriated. "Ummm, hello girls! This is an amazing step for us, can't you see that? We may not have it all figured out, but I know this isn't a fling. You're forgetting that you're talking to the queen of flings, so I would know if I was one!" she continued.

"Okay, so what happens with your life...the one you built here in D.C.? Everything you've accumulated, the friendships you've made, your career, the apartment that we share...what happens to us?" I questioned out of both curiosity and fear. No one was ever really sure about this Garrett character of hers. He was known for being a player and he was always on the party scene with a different girl on his arm every week. I didn't want to see Josey give up her entire world for a man that wouldn't be willing to do the same for her.

"This is too much! I just...I...don't know! I don't have all the answers, okay! Call me crazy, but I thought that when I came over here to share this life changing news with you guys that you all would, I don't know, be happy for me!" Josey's frustration seemed to cloud her thoughts. She paused for a moment wiping away a tear from her watery eyes before it could fall down her cheek. "I just wanted you guys to support me...and...just be happy for me! I'm in love! Just be happy for me, please!"

We looked around at each other in silence for a few moments before I asked, "Listen Josey, we are happy for you, but what kind of friends would we be if we didn't share our concerns?"

"Good ones! The kind that would be happy for me instead of being jealous!" she blurted out grabbing her purse and coat before we could respond. "You know what? Just forget it..." Josey grumbled as she continued to walk away.

"We're sorry! Sit down! We want to celebrate this milestone with you!" Gia pleaded.

"Gia is right, we're sorry! This is great news, please, just sit back down!" Taylor added.

"Then stop spoiling this moment for me with all these damn questions," Josey demands as she turned back.

"We just want to make sure you're making the right decision, J! This all happened so quickly, it just caught us by surprise. Plus, can you blame us for being mad that he's taking you from us all the way to the other side of the country!" Gia joked, trying to ease the tension.

"I have thought this through, Gia. You don't think this is going to be hard for me too? But I'm willing to sacrifice stepping away from my familiar, comfortable life for a chance at love...I'm afraid that if I pass this chance up...that..." she stopped, wiping her nose then slowly continued, "that it may not come again. I've never felt like this before. And you guys know me; I'm not used to feeling anything in my relationships."

"Then Josey, we're happy that you're happy," Taylor said.

Josey could sense the disingenuous vibe in our words. An awkward silence fell over the group once again as we sat there picking at the appetizers I had prepared that night.

"You know, I think I'm going to go. I have some things to take care of for Garrett before his game tomorrow," Josey said walking out on a conversation we never spoke of again, even after all these years.

Two weeks later Garrett's season ended and as planned, Josey moved her entire life to Los Angeles without knowing a single sole. She left her job, her family, her home, and she left us. Our relationship suffered for the better part of a year because she was initially all consumed with Garrett, but once his season got back into full swing, she came around. We never quite got back to where we were in our friendship. Josey just didn't seem as open as she once was, seemingly in an effort to project that everything was good at home and within her relationship, but we all knew better.

———

To my own surprise I pulled into the valet of The Beacon Hotel early, exactly five minutes before eleven. As soon as I walk into the lobby, Josey greets me draped in a flowing lime green maxi dress with snakeskin Gucci sandals. We warmly embrace each other for a few moments before heading into the dining area. We're directed to a table reserved to hold the four of us, once the other ladies join us a little later.

As we sip on our mimosas, Josey inquires, "So, how are things going with Jay?"

Unable to tame my smile I respond, "Great! Things have been going a little faster than I'm used to, but I'm enjoying every minute of it."

"That's good to hear! I keep forgetting to ask Garrett if he knows Jay.

You know these football and basketball leagues are small honey, can't have you running around with a playboy because you know how they can be!" Josey says, shaking her head as she sips from her champagne glass.

"Speaking of...so what's been going on with you and your hubby? We haven't seen much of you since your wedding last spring, which I have to say again was amazing!"

"Oh thanks, Dee!" exhaling, she stops for a moment, falling back in her seat as sadness falls over her. "Girl, honestly...it's been a struggle. That's why I wanted to talk to you before the girls came. You know, I think I was incredibly naive in thinking that marriage would be a cure for a lot of our issues...that it would make him come home at night. But not much has changed." Looking down, she adds, "I wish our marriage was as beautiful as the wedding."

"Wow, I'm sorry to hear that. Is it the partying and staying out that's bothering you?" I ask.

"It's not just the excessive partying. I knew I married a party boy, I just thought taking vows in front of God would make him be faithful and make him want to be a better, more responsible man. Instead, he's just gotten craftier with his cheating, but I know there are other women."

"Women?" I ask, making sure I heard her right.

"Yes, plural. As in more than one," she clarifies.

"Josey, how long has this been going on?" I inquire.

"For way longer than I'd like to admit. I just got so used to turning the other cheek and ignoring things that just didn't sit well with me. I guess I was just so ashamed to tell you guys what was really going on; ashamed to admit that you guys were right. I gave up my entire life for him, and now it feels like he is my life. My entire life revolves around a man," Josey admits as her eyes start to water.

"Josey, you know you can come to us. We're not here to judge you! We just want you to be okay. And if it's not with him, then it doesn't make you weak or a failure to walk away and admit that you made a mistake," I explain.

"I just feel like such a fool, Dee! I don't know how I let this happen to me! Now I'm the girl that we used to shake our heads at. The girl who knows her man is no good, but doesn't complain as long as he's keeping her laced in Gucci and commas in her bank account. I can't believe I sold into this lifestyle, and for what? Some damn overpriced purses and shoes that are going to be out of style in five minutes? I don't know what I'm doing with my life anymore. What happened to me?" Trying to compose herself, she wipes away her tears and takes a deep breath before continuing, "I feel like I've completely lost myself and I don't know how to get her back. She isn't me anymore because the person I am now, I don't even recognize." Josey pauses again, this time looking around hoping no one was watching as she dabs the corners of her eyes. "I'm sorry Dee, I'm so embarrassed."

"You don't have anything to be embarrassed about," I say, grabbing her hand. "Look on the bright side; you're moving in the right direction now! Instead of pretending and putting on a facade like everything's perfect, you're taking control of your life and consciously choosing a better quality of life. You may not be able to have a new $3,000 Chanel purse every season, but you won't have to continually waste your days drowning in tears and playing detective over Garrett's infidelity. We've all been there! You know we'll help you get through this and figure it out! Promise!" She grabs my hand tighter, thanking me for supporting her. I just want her to be happy again and get back to being the vibrant woman that I met all those years ago because, truth be told, I don't recognize the woman she's become either.

I sit back in my seat sipping the last of my mimosa, hoping that Josey was really ready. I've been through these talks before with her when she hinted at his wrong doing, but two weeks later she would be back to playing like nothing ever happened. I wondered if this would be a lifelong game of charades for her or if she was finally ready to step out on faith and know that she's better than the situation she's settling for. It's easy to say you want to walk away, just like it's easy for Garrett to constantly claim change, but the hardest part always lies in the actions that follow. If he can't get right and stay right, then I fully encourage Josey to go left and get her life and herself back.

CHAPTER 9

"Well, hello strangers!" Taylor calls out. Josey and I turn to greet her as she approaches the table.

"It feels like we haven't seen you in ages! I miss my friend, my sister!" Taylor says as she pulls Josey in for a firm hug, as if she sensed that she needed it.

"And you..." Taylor looks my direction, "Where have you been, woman? And don't say work, unless you're referring to that 180 pounds of pure chocolate muscle of a man you've been hold up with lately! In that case, you're excused!" We all burst into laughter at Taylor's lack of a filter. "As much as I love y'all, I don't blame you girl because I would get ghost on y'all too if I found a good man!" she continues as she sits down across from me.

"Guilty! Jay has definitely been getting a lot of my time lately, and I can't say that I regret it. We're still in the honeymoon phase, so you know I'm trying to ride that out as long as possible," I jokingly reply.

Just as the waiter comes to refill our mimosas, Gia arrives. We all stand to hug and greet her. None of us could suppress our happiness and excitement to be back together. It had been almost a year since all of us were able to be in the same place at the same time. There was always someone who would miss one of our regular get togethers because of a conflict of schedule, but we were determined to get back on track.

"So..." Gia jumps right into conversation after we ravish the brunch buffet and sit back down at our table. "I hear someone at this table has gotten themselves a man and has neglected to give her girls all of the details!" she proceeds to fake cough and call me out.

"Well, you know I'm not one to brag, but I finally hit the love jackpot!" I exclaim.

"Okay! I want to hear it all! How did y'all meet? How long has this been going on? Does he have any kids? Does he have a job...you know, the legal kind where taxes get taken out of his check? What does..." Taylor rattles off her list of questions, before Josey interrupts, "Damn 50 Cent! If you would calm down with your 21 questions, maybe she could actually answer one of them!"

"Okay Dee, spill the tea already!" Gia adds.

Barely able to control my laughter, I begin to give the girls a little background and insight into my new relationship with Jay. I've been holding back because I wanted to be sure that this was a relationship with a future and not another disappointment. Before Jay, I went through a string of dating situations with men for years where I felt like they could potentially be husband material, only to be devastated a few months into it when I find out they were nothing to be excited about. And there's nothing worse than telling your girlfriends about Prince Charming one week, and by week three you're back to kissing a frog. The worst!

Seeking to appease all of their questions, I begin to tell them about how I came to meet Jay.

"Okay, so you all remember Chase, right?"

"The party promoter, slash hustler, slash manager — the child with all the jobs?" Gia jokingly responds.

"Yeah, that Chase!" I confirm. "I was helping Sophie, from work, pack up her apartment a few months ago when Chase called and invited us out. We had been packing all day and really needed a break, so we agreed."

"Oh, Lord! Don't tell me he had you up in some raunchy club, Dee!" Taylor says.

"Let me say this...it wasn't the plan, but you know how well Chase sticks to those! We were supposed to go to some hookah spot down the street but somehow ended up at this cute little lounge downtown for his friend's birthday party. We weren't supposed to stick around for too long, but once we got there, it was actually really nice so we decided to stay. Long story short, you know how those cheesy guys come around with the basket of roses, trying to guilt all the guys into buying them for their ladies? Well, Sophie was being silly and waived the guy over to buy me a dozen roses as a thank you for helping her pack up her apartment. We laughed it off until this handsome guy comes and sits next to me and waves the flower guy back over. He buys me two dozen roses and tells me that anything she can do, referring to Sophie, he could do it better...and Mr. Handsome turned out to be Jay!"

"Dee, stop! That has got to be the corniest shit I have ever heard!" Josey blurts out.

"Trust me, I know! But if it didn't get better, that would be the end of this story!" I explain. "He sat down and we started talking and I found out that it was actually his birthday that Chase was coming to celebrate. We only got to speak briefly, of course, because how much can you say in a crowded lounge with music blaring? But I really enjoyed how effortless our conversation was and how immediately I felt comfortable with him, so when he asked if he could take me on a date, I agreed and we exchanged numbers. So a couple days later he calls me and asks if he can take me out to dinner the next evening.

First of all, when he called and said he would have his driver come and pick me up and take me to the restaurant, I was a little taken aback."

"A driver? Girl, who are you dating? You got mini Donald Trump over there?" Taylor sarcastically questions.

Laughing in unison, Josey responds, "Okay Kevin Hart with the jokes today! If you would withhold your commentary, we can find out!" Shifting her focus back to me, "Continue, girl! We're just going to ignore Taylor for now!"

Trying to regain my focus, "Okay, where'd I stop?"

"With the driver, girl! Focus!" Taylor reminds me.

"Oh, yeah! So, we arrived at this really nice waterfront restaurant in Georgetown as the sun is setting. Jay is standing there all smiles with a nice navy blazer on with a white, collared shirt and white dress pants. He comes to open my door then leads me to the table hand in hand. I follow him up to the second floor balcony to a table set with the perfect view of the water. We sat there and talked for hours! Dinner was just as amazing as our conversation."

"That's cute and all, but what's the dirt? Kids? Age? We need the goods!" Taylor interrupts again.

"I'm trying to get there!" I roll my eyes at her impatience. "So he told me that he was 33, no kids, hasn't been in any serious relationships because of work, but that he is finally at a point in life where he wants to settle down and have a family. I just remember thinking to myself that this was it! By the end of the date I felt like this could really be the one! The chemistry was there and this may be the first time I have ever heard a guy plainly state that he was seeking a serious relationship, instead of the usual, 'let's just see where this goes' BS."

"Wait, pause! So what does he do?" Gia asks.

"Well, that's sort of the downside. He plays professionally for the local football team, which was something that made me a little apprehensive."

"Uhhh! Don't do it, girl! No offense, Josey," Taylor says, "but you know exactly how that story goes! Hell, we all do! And the ending is never good."

"I hate to say it, but I kind of agree with Taylor on this one. But who knows, maybe he is in that small percentage that has the ability to be faithful!" Trying to sound hopeful, Gia only reinforces my fear.

Josey sat there avoiding eye contact with anyone, reacting as if this topic was hitting way too close to home. I attempt to reassure the girls that although this is a new relationship, Jay has shown all the signs that he was mature enough to actually be the person he claims to be.

"You guys should give him a chance! It's been a few months and we've been inseparable since our first date. He's been nothing but reliable and honest with me. I actually trust him and you guys know how hard it is for me to trust men! We talk via face time, over the phone, or by text every single day and I've even met his mom! Now tell me those aren't signs that a man is serious about his word!"

"I'll give you that one, Dee! He sounds pretty amazing. Just give it some time and see if this really pans out before you invest too much of yourself," Josey advises.

The girls shake their head in agreement. I felt the conversation getting a little heavy, so I decide to change the tone of the conversation and tell the girls my other big news. "Oh, I forgot to mention that I saw my father this weekend while I was in Chicago."

"No! How did that go?" Taylor asks.

"Terrible at first, but he eventually ended up meeting me at my hotel and apologizing for his absence and asking that I allow him to be a part of my life again. I don't know how big of a part I want him to play just yet, but he gave me a lot to think about. He even gave me some pretty sound advice on Tate, even though I didn't ask for it."

Josey was furious just at the mention of his name. "Tate? How did that fool come up? Don't tell me you're opening that door again!"

"No! Actually I closed that door, locked it, and threw away the key for good."

"I was about to say, Dee! You had us worried."

"But I did see him randomly," I admit.

Smacking her lips, Taylor responds, "So how did that meeting come about? Is he living in Chicago or just out there with one of his flings cheating on his wife?"

"No. It wasn't like that. He saw me when I was leaving the airport and kept calling me trying to talk. I finally agreed to it, but I thought he stood me up, so I invited my father over to talk instead. Once he left, Tate saw my father and thought he was someone I was dating. He told me he was late because he was helping his mom out with something for a house she was purchasing and we talked for a few." The look of concern and disappointment was all over the girls' faces. "Nothing happened! He did mention that he got a divorce though...I'm sure he thought that was enough to win me back, but I shut down any glimmer of hope. I made it clear that I moved on. Then he left, and that was that."

"Whew! Good. I remember the days when a lack luster apology from his lips one moment would lead to your panties around your ankles the next!" Taylor so abruptly reminds us.

"Yeah, that was then and this is now! You gotta work a lot harder these days for the panties!" I joke.

"Oh, is that right? So you're going to tell me Jay hasn't gotten any yet?" Josey interjects.

"So, yeah, about my father..." I attempt to change the subject without admitting my guilt to the girls.

"Uh huh! We knew it!" they all join in on the joke, laughing in sync.

We sat and talked about all that happened in Chicago in detail before kissing each other good-bye and going our separate ways, agreeing to stick to our next meet up in a couple months.

As soon as the valet took my ticket, I heard my cell phone chiming repeatedly in my purse. Unsurprisingly, it's my mother. I'm sure she just wants to be nosey and find out how things went with my father, as if she hasn't already asked him and found out before calling. I know her too well.

"Hey Ma!"

"Hey baby! How was your flight home?"

"It was good. I almost missed it staying up kind of late talking to Robert."

"Oh and how did that go? Assuming you used your manners this time..."

"I did my best!" I pause for a moment as the valet pulls my car forward and get in. "I think we may have made some headway, but we definitely have a long road ahead of us. I, uhhh...I broke down a little bit when we were talking and it made me realize how angry I was and how much hurt and anger I've been carrying around. I don't want to be that person anymore so I left all those negative emotions at the table that night. I just hope he doesn't disappoint me again. I need him to be genuine and really be there for me this time."

"I know this was hard for you, but I'm proud of you. I'm proud that you had the courage to come and face this situation instead of holding onto the pain and anger and allow it to eat you up. The real reason I was so adamant about you coming to meet with your father is because I too had to take responsibility for my role in this. Even though I felt like taking you and your brother and starting over was the best thing, I came the realize that no matter how amazing of a mom I am, there are certain things that he can give you that I just can't. Bottom line is, you can go another 20 years wondering what your father should have told you or you can open your heart to what he can teach you now. It's never too late to lighten the load of a heavy heart, and it's clear that the lack of a relationship with your father is the root of a lot of what's been weighing you down."

"You're right, Ma. If he's willing to make the effort, the least I can do is meet him half way."

My mother's comments left me reflecting on all of the times I wished my father had been around when it came to the knuckleheads I dated. And I dated them all—from Mr. Too Busy, Mr. Gotta Lie to Kick It to Mr. Oh, I Forgot I Was Married!

"Be open, that's all I ask. It's not going to happen overnight, baby, but I get the feeling that he won't be pulling any disappearing acts this go round. It may have taken a couple decades, but by God, he seems to have finally gotten it right."

"I hope so...I really do."

"If it's God's will, it'll be."

"I agree. Listen Ma, I hopped right off the plane to come to brunch with the girls. Now that it's over, I'm heading home to get some rest. I'm so exhausted, so I'm gonna call you back a little later. Okay?"

"Okay, baby. Get some rest. Love you!"

"Love you, too," I say, before hanging up.

The 20 minute drive home of uninterrupted silence was the most peace I had gotten all weekend. Unfortunately, that was all the time that I would get to myself before my phone went off again. This time it was Jay asking me to come over to his house in a few. So much for that nap...

TASHA RAY

CHAPTER 10

Later that evening, I find myself standing in Jay's kitchen looking out of the broad floor to ceiling windows lining the entire back wall of his mansion, overlooking his backyard. In his oversized button front pajama top, I turn and yell out, "Do you realize we haven't used your hot tub yet?"

Closing the refrigerator door, he turns and looks at me with a grin. "You thinking what I'm thinking?"

"Yep, beat you to it! Loser makes dinner!" I hurriedly yell out over my shoulder as we both rush towards the basement steps leading to the hot tub in the backyard.

Before I know it, Jay is right behind me tugging at my top and trying to pull me behind him so that he can win the bet. Laughing uncontrollably at his blatant cheating tactics, he tickles and nudges me out of his way as we finally make it around the swimming pool to the hot tub.

"And I still won, you little cheater!" I yell out, falling onto the side ledge of the hot tub trying to catch my breath.

"It's only because I'm a gentleman! I let you win!" he says with a grin.

"Oh, okay! In that case, I'm gonna let you make me dinner tonight too since you're such a gentleman!"

Smiling, Jay comes closer to me and embraces me as we sit with our feet resting in the hot tub. "So are you getting in?" he questions, with a smirk. "It's just us two! No one else is going to see your birthday suit out here!"

"If I recall correctly, you're the one who lost the bet! And losers always have to go first!" I tease back.

"You're right! You win again." He stands up, drops his basketball shorts to his ankles, and hops in. "Now it's your turn!"

Caught by surprise, I unbutton each button of the plaid pajama top slowly before joining him in the steamy, bubbly waters. It was so quiet and serene. All I could hear was the sound of the water bubbling as I look up into the dark sky and get lost in the starry night. The moon was full and the stars were so bright and clear. We were surrounded by nothing but nature, without a neighboring house in sight. Noticing how mesmerized I was by the peacefulness of the night, I catch Jay staring at me in amusement through the corner of my eye. "That's why you have to get out of the city sometimes, baby. No sirens or noisy neighbors—-just us and the night sky."

"You're right. Bracing the Virginia traffic just might be worth coming home to this peace and quiet every night." Catching myself, I try to recover, "I mean, not your house per se, just...you know, Virginia...outside of the city." Fumble. That wasn't much of a recovery.

To my surprise, Jay responds, "Hmmm...I think you had it right the first time. I wouldn't mind you coming home every night to this peace and quiet either." He pulls me in close to him with our naked bodies flush against one another and kisses my forehead continuously.

"You make me feel so lucky. Sometimes I wonder if you can really understand how much I care for you and how deeply I'm falling for you," he says, staring into my eyes as his hands grasp both sides of my face. "I think sometimes other people have a way of expressing how I feel, better than I can." Jay turns and reaches into the pocket of his shorts and pulls out his cell phone. A few moments later, John Legend's "You and I" plays from the sound system connected to the outdoor pool area.

I close my eyes and take in every second of this magical moment. Jay comes back and embraces me and all I can do was hug him harder. I couldn't find the words to explain how much my heart was truly smiling. With my head resting on his chest, he explains, "When I heard this song, I thought about you. You're so beautiful and sometimes when I tell you, I wonder if you actually believe me." Pulling my chin away from his chest and looking into my eyes, he continues, "I want you to believe me because I mean every word I say to you. Just being around you brings out the joy in me, no matter what other chaos is going on around me. When you're here and I'm holding you, nothing else seems to matter. I've never been good at this, but I'll do whatever it takes to make sure this feeling never fades."

His eyes start to tear up, which brought me even more joy to know that there was true emotion and feeling behind his words. I kiss him softly and continue caressing his back as we stare at each other in admiration listening to soft, sensual melodic tunes, getting lost in the moment.

"Alright, now that we're all shriveled up," I say jokingly, "let's go shower then swing by the grocery store so I can get ready to enjoy this great meal you're about to prepare."

"Oh, I was hoping you forgot!" laughing as we exit the hot tub, he comes up and hugs me from behind. He whispers in my ear, "I love you." Turning back and looking up at him, I whisper back, "I love you, too...and if you can really cook, I'll love you even more after dinner!" Shaking his head, giggling, he smacks my butt as we head back into the house.

We race up the spiral staircase into his room, when he turns and pulls me in firmly against his wet, naked body while slowly kissing my neck. He wraps his arms around me, guiding me into the adjacent bathroom without letting go. Jay slung open the glass shower door and turns the knobs until warm water begins sprouting out from the shower head directly above us. Water pours down our bodies as if we were standing directly beneath a waterfall as Jay starts to wash my back from behind. Gently, he lathers the vanilla scented body wash all over my body beginning with my shoulders then gradually working his way down all the way down to my feet. Closing my eyes, my mind drifts out of pure bliss at how amazing of a man I've been so fortunate to find.

Jay had it all. He was breathtakingly handsome and highly educated. His body was sculpted to perfection with abs that Picasso could have chiseled himself, his sense of humor was infectious, and he has a blossoming professional football career that allows him to live a lavish lifestyle. I'm not sure that a package gets any better than this when it comes to men these days.

Although Jay's life seemed picture perfect on the outside, his past was nothing of the sort. He grew up in Southeast D.C. in a time and place where drugs were running rampant and destroying neighborhoods. Violence was a constant and he confided in me many times that he was often unsure of if he would make it out of the city that made him, alive. Thankfully, his grandmother didn't allow him to fail and succumb to his surroundings. She pushed him to go to college on a full scholarship and made sure he stayed away from the city and out of trouble until he graduated and was eventually drafted into the football league. Though she did her best to create distance from his past and the future that was ahead of him, Jay felt like a sell out for leaving to play professionally in Florida while the few childhood friends of his that were still alive, lived in such poor conditions. He knew he was blessed to make it out and see life from a different perspective, which changed his outlook on life, all the while the friends who supported him were stuck in the same cycle of drugs, jail, and violence. He started to feel like if he could just bring them out of their norm, that they would see life the way he did and eventually evolve too.

But Jay's childhood friends became adult leeches, eventually following him to every new city he went to for work with their hands out. Things only got worse when he decided to come back home and play for the team he grew up cheering for and idolizing, but being home came with its own brand new set of problems. Though he was living out his dream professionally, his personal life was rapidly becoming nothing short of a nightmare. The women, the money, and the long lost family members all made life hectic for him and sometimes pushed him out of character. It seemingly brought out the anger that he successfully suppressed over the years. He learned to internalize his problems at a young age, which resulted in unpredictable outbursts of anger. I hated to see him lose his temper, but I understood where it came from. I justified it to myself and wanted to be that escape from the chaos for him because inadvertently he's been that for me.

CHAPTER 11

"Hello?"

"Hey Dee, are you busy?" Josey asks.

"Hey girl, I'm just at the store with Jay picking up a few things for dinner. Why, what's up?" I ask.

"Maybe this isn't the best time then. Why don't you call me when you get home?"

"Josey, stop it! What's going on? Just tell me now!"

"It's about Jay."

"Okay, what about him?" I nervously respond, walking to the end of the aisle in the opposite direction of where he's standing.

"I asked Garrett if he knew Jay, and he said he does. Turns out they have a few friends in common from the time Garrett played in D.C. and I happen to know one of their wives really well, so I gave her a call. We talked for a bit and she told me some things about Jay that made me question his intentions with you. Now I'm not trying to stir anything up, I just want you to talk with him about this and make sure there's nothing more to the story."

"Okay, Josey. Please stop beating around the bush!"

"Alright! She was telling me the last time they saw him earlier this year, he brought another woman around."

"Don't tell me he's married!"

"No, no! Well, I don't think so. But just ask him what his relationship is with a woman named Tori. I'm going to leave it at that, because if there is more to the story, he should be the one to tell it."

"Really, Josey? You're not going to tell me the whole story!"

"No, Dee! It's not my place. As your best friend, I've done my part. I'll at least give him the chance to man up. Hopefully, he can clear things up and there won't even be an issue. Just talk to him tonight and call me later. Okay?"

"Okay. I'll see what he has to say. Bye."

Josey's call left me really shaken up and in the dark. I don't know when the appropriate time to ask him about this is, especially since I don't even know what I can expect to hear come out of his mouth. I decide to walk back into the aisle where Jay is crouched over, picking out all of the ingredients for some Jambalaya recipe that I'm sure he found at the last minute on Pinterest. I just let him act like he really knows how to cook so I can take advantage of having the night off in the kitchen.

"Hey babe, who was that on the phone?" he asks.

"Oh, just one of my girlfriends." Still bothered by my conversation with Josey, I suggest, "Come on, let's get the rest of these groceries and go to the car."

"Okay, is everything alright? Your mood just shifted a little bit."

Being very short with him, I respond, "I'm okay."

Hesitant to respond, he says, "Okay...you sure?"

"Yep, let's go."

On the ride home, the conversation I had with Josey was starting to eat at me. I finally decide to turn to Jay and find out what part of the story she was neglecting to tell me.

"Jay, do you feel like you've been totally honest with me?"

"Oh Lord, where is this going?" he asks, defensively.

"Just answer me."

"Yes. I've been honest with you, Dulsey."

"Well then, who is Tori?"

All of a sudden Jay's usual joking demeanor shifts to a blank stare. We sat there in an uncomfortable silence for several moments before he pulls over on the side of the dark country road. The silence continues as I wait for his response, then all of a sudden a tear starts to stream down his cheek. He drops his head down into his hands, wiping the tears away with both hands, leaving me utterly confused and speechless. He then sits back in his seat, looking straightforward out of the front window instead of looking at me.

"I feel like every time something good happens to me, a dumb decision from my past always comes back around and messes things up," he says in a barely audible voice. Taking a deep breath, he further explains, "Tori is someone I know from high school. We hadn't seen each other in years but reconnected through mutual friends when I moved back here last year. After I broke up with my last girlfriend, we dated for a little bit...if you can even really call it that." He's slow to continue talking, then starts to fiddle with his hands before he finally adds, "She...ummm...she contacted me recently and told me that she's pregnant." Before I could react, he turns towards me and tries to explain further, "But I don't think the baby is mine! I think she sees me as a big pay day, so she's trying to pin this baby on me!"

Astounded by what I'm hearing, I fall back into my seat and turn my back to him as I gaze out of the window trying to make sense of things. After several minutes of being unresponsive to his attempts to talk, he grows frustrated and finally pulls back onto the road as we ride the entire way back to his house in silence.

As we approach his driveway, he says serenely, "Dulsey, I'm really sorry. I'm sorry that this is how you had to hear this...you didn't deserve to find out like this."

"So when did you plan to tell me, huh? After she had the baby?" shaking my head in disbelief, "Or did you ever plan to tell me at all?"

He was silent.

I got out of the car, slamming the door behind me with the intentions of getting my keys out of the house and driving home. Jay enters the house behind me, following my every move. "Please stay! At least stay for dinner so we can talk about this more!"

"I'm not sure there is anything else to talk about, Jay."

I retrieve my keys and head back towards the garage to leave when Jay steps in front of me, slamming his hand against the wall blocking the doorway. Startling me, his temper starts to flare.

"Jay, please! Let's not do this. I really just want to go right now!"

Regretful of his aggression, he pulls his arm back resting his head against the wall. "I know and I'm sorry! But running away isn't going to fix this." He turns and grabs my hand, pleading, "Let me try to make this right! Please, just hear me out!"

Unable to get a hold over my emotions any longer, I break down into tears. Jay catches me as I fall to my knees in grief.

"Why didn't you tell me?" I scream out through my tears while pounding on his chest as he holds me tighter. He picks me up and carries me into the living room. Still cradling me in his arms, he sits me down on the couch and kneels down on the floor in front of me so that we're face to face.

"I hate that you allowed me to fall in love with this idea of who I thought you were! This makes me question everything. I'm not sure if I even know who you really are! If you hid something so major, why wouldn't you be capable of lying about other things?" I inquire, angrily. "So, how far along is she?"

Clearing his throat, he looks around before answering, "About four months."

"Did you know she was pregnant before we went on our first date?"

"Ummm...yeah, I did. I found out around that time."

Still in shock, "I don't think I can trust you, and if I can't trust you, we can't be together."

"Dulsey, we just shared the most amazing night together! All of that was real and still is. I made a mistake — one that I will regret forever if I lose you. Please, don't give up on me now!"

I stop for a moment to gather my thoughts.

"I'm sorry. I just...I can't."

I stood up, grabbed my keys and headed out of the door. I sat in his driveway for several minutes trying to get myself together long enough to make it home, but the tears wouldn't stop flowing. My frustration grew greater and anger started to take over. Trying to find the balance, I knew I needed to get this out and vent to someone. I shuffled around in my purse for my cell phone to call Taylor just as I backed out of his driveway and drove back towards the city.

"Taylor, can you meet me at my house?"

"Sure! Elijah is spending the night with one of his friends from school, so I can be there in thirty minutes. Is everything okay?"

"I'll tell you about it when you get there. Your detective skills are needed. Oh, and bring some wine."

"Honey, say no more. See you soon!"

If anyone could help me feel better in this moment, it was Taylor. I need answers and not the sugar coated, half-assed kind that would have come out of Jay's mouth if I had given him the chance. I need to know everything there is to know about him and his possible baby's mother in order to have a conversation with Jay. I need to be equipped with the truth so that I'll know how honest he is, and Taylor is just the woman to get it for me. If there's dirt to be found, she will scour the entire internet until she finds it.

Halfway home, I look down to see my father calling. Crying and still not in the best shape, I accidentally press the answer button instead of ending the call. Having answered in error, I try to quickly brush him off, "Hey Robert, this isn't a good time."

Hearing the hurt in my voice, he inquires, "What's wrong, baby girl? Did you have a bad day at work or something?"

"No, more like a bad day in my love life."

"Ahhh, I see. Sweetie, I think this is the part where you let me be dad. You see, there's one thing I know, and that's a man. The good, bad, and the ugly because I've been there, done that and sold every dream possible to more women than I can remember. So is this about that Tate fellow you were telling me about?"

"Oh, no! Tate is history. I'm having issues with a guy named Jay that I've been dating for the last few months. He...umm..." pausing, I found it difficult to even get the words out without breaking down again.

"It's okay, sweetie! Take your time."

Taking a deep breath, I was finally able to get the words out. "I found out today that he may have fathered a child. On top of that, the only reason I found out was because one of my girlfriends tipped me off. I'm not sure if he would have ever told me if she hadn't."

"I'm so sorry to hear that, baby girl."

"I'm just so sick of ending up with jerks and selfish assholes that never once consider my feelings. It's so hard to find someone who is genuine these days and I feel like my time is running out!"

"It's never too late! But what are you going to do now?"

"Well, my girlfriend Taylor is in route to my house right now to get all the dirt on him and this other woman. I want to know all the facts before I confront him so he won't have the opportunity to get over on me again with a lie."

"Now you know you don't need to do that! If you go looking for something, you're going to find it. And when you do, it's going to hurt you even more! You've got to give him a chance to come clean before you nail him to the cross."

"Robert, I know. You make perfect sense, but me, my tears, and my broken heart don't want to hear that right now," I say trying to defend my juvenile actions.

"One thing you may not want to hear but that you need to understand is that it's not your will, it's God's. So if something or someone is for you, nothing will hold you from your destiny. But help me to understand, is it over for you because there is a baby or because he wasn't upfront about it?" Robert asks.

"Listen, Robert. I'm not living in a fairy tale. I know that at my age, it's pretty damn hard to find someone who doesn't have kids. I'm usually just hoping that there aren't multiple by more than one woman! I can't be upset with him over a choice he made before we even knew each other existed, however I can be every bit of pissed off that he mislead me all this time. He knew when we met that he may have a child on the way, and still passed himself off as this poor single guy with no kids who has just been unlucky in love. I don't take kindly to being played for a fool when I'm giving myself to him fully and being open and honest with every question he's asked!" I explain. "I just don't know what I'm doing wrong!"

"Well, it sounds to me that you made the mistake that a lot of women make who just want to be loved. You're giving too much of yourself too soon! How long have you been dating this guy?"

"A few months," I admit.

"That's the problem! Before you give yourself to a man fully, you have to give the relationship time to blossom and see what that person is really like after the honeymoon phase wears off. What's done in the dark is bound to come to the light in due time. Now is this the football player or the business man your mom told me about?"

"I see mom is still telling all my business to anyone who will listen...but he's the football player."

"Yeah, with guys like that, you have to be twice as careful. You have a man who is used to getting what he wants, when he wants it. You have to set the standard for him, and if he really wants you he'll live up to it. But most importantly, you need to set standards for yourself and not be so quick to accept someone else's baggage out of fear that you'll be alone or won't find someone better."

"I know. It's just so hard to deny what feels natural sometimes. Even though I always want to take it slow, somehow I get caught up in the moment and give in."

"What is it that you really want, that you absolutely need? And before you list anything, you have to know and believe that you deserve it! And once you believe it and implement it, I guarantee you'll stop putting the cart before the horse when you see how many heartbreaks you'll avoid by just pacing yourself."

"I guess I never really thought about it like that. I've spent so much time trying to please men and prove to them that I'm worthy, that I never thought about what I needed in return."

"If you've never figured out what you need and have no expectations, a man doesn't have a level of standards to live up to. But if you don't know it already, you deserve a solid God-fearing man who would never gamble with your heart. Take your time and be patient. I know the right one will find you."

"Thanks...Dad. You really put things into perspective for me. I appreciate this. I actually feel a little better!"

"But let me guess, you're still going to snoop, huh?" he says, laughing to himself.

"Yep! You must've been keeping tabs on me all these years, because you have me pegged!"

My father really got me thinking about the choices I've made when it comes to men. I realize now that I really need to develop some boundaries for men so that I won't keep falling into these ridiculous situations. Had I taken my time, maybe I would've learned about the pregnancy before I developed feelings and told Jay that I love him. Maybe then it wouldn't hurt so bad and I wouldn't need to go snooping for the truth. But with all that aside, Taylor arrives just in time to help me get to the bottom of who Jay really is. If there's dirt to be found, Taylor will find it!

CHAPTER 12

Palming a bottle of chardonnay, Taylor follows me through the front door. Before we could even get in the house, the questions are already starting to roll off of her tongue. Answering her right away wasn't my first priority — wine was. She follows me into the kitchen waiting to find out why I asked her over as I pop the cork on the bottle of wine. Pouring us both a glass, I let her know about the "maybe baby" on the way. Stunned, we both sat across from each other at the dining room table in silence for a moment as if we needed to let the overwhelming information sink in.

"It just doesn't feel real, Taylor!" I confess.

"Girl, I am so sorry. I really had high hopes for this one, especially the way you were gushing over him just the other day. I hadn't seen you so happy with a man in such a long time."

"Ugh, don't remind me. And the crazy part is he'd just told me that he loved me for the first time right before I found out about this entire situation. I really wish I would've waited instead of getting caught up in the excitement of it all in the beginning. That way I might at least be walking away from this knowing that I hadn't given my time, effort, and my body to someone who didn't deserve it in the first place." Exhaling in regret, "I'm such an idiot! I'm too old to be making the same mistakes that I made in my twenties."

"Oh, Dee, now calm down! You're being entirely too hard on yourself. You can't blame yourself for believing that someone just so happened to be who they portrayed themselves to be. I know it's rare these days, but you can't be upset with yourself for trusting your heart and believing that he could actually be a man of his word," stopping briefly to sip her drink, she continues, "but this is why I don't even give 'em the time of day. Getting attached in today's world is a waste of time. It's just a set up to get your heart broken with all these confused, broken little men running around getting their relationship advice from rap songs. But anyway, shall we snoop now?" Taylor openly suggests with a smirk.

"Sadly, I think that might make me feel better! Maybe it'll shed some light on who I've really been sharing a bed with all this time."

"Or better yet, who else he's been sharing his bed with," Taylor adds.

I can't help but to shake my head at the thought of him being intimate with another woman at the same time as me.

"Okay, first things first. What's the girl's name? We can start with that."

"Josey told me her name was Tori. I'm not sure what her last name is."

"Perfect. Don't need it! Tori is enough." Taylor scrolls through his social media pages searching for any clues that could lead us to Tori, when she finally stops to look a bit harder at the screen.

"What is it?" I question.

"I think I found her! And the chick ain't even cute!" Taylor exclaims.

"Are they ever?" I mumble, falling back in my chair unsure of if I really wanted to see who could possibly be carrying Jay's child.

"Girl, come over here and check this out. I think Jay has a bit more explaining to do because from what you told me, his dates aren't adding up." As I walk around to peek over Taylor's shoulder, she says, "This is a prime example of why you should have a social media page. If your man has a page, oh honey, you need a page too! How else are you going to keep tabs and make sure he's behaving?"

"Trust, Taylor. That's how!"

"Well, we see how far trust got you," she says sarcastically.

Biting my lip, "Point taken."

Taylor and I dissected Jay and Tori's pages for the next hour, which only led to more confusion. Apparently, from the dates of the pictures Tori posted with Jay's house in the background, they were very much still involved. We even found out that she has a child already and that Jay was a part of the little boy's life in some way, as he was present in a few group shots that were from several months prior. As if this situation couldn't get any messier, a name caught my eye in the comment section under one of his older pictures.

"Wait, wait, wait! Scroll back up. Click on this girl, Morgan's name. That sounds so familiar. Jay never mentioned the ex-girlfriend that he lived with briefly by name, but his driver slipped up and said it a couple weeks ago. I think this might be her."

As soon as the page opens up, we both look at each other scoffing at the screen in disbelief.

"Hold on, his ex is a stripper?" Taylor yells out, "Mmm, with bad plastic surgery too. Yuck!"

"I'm gonna have a seat. I don't...I don't think I can take much more. I feel like I don't even know who this man is. It's like I've been dating a stranger!"

"Oh, okay. Well, you go have a seat then. Don't mind me; I'm just going to check this chick out a little further. She seems to be an attention whore, putting all of her business out there for the world to see. Whew! Thank God for silly people like this, they keep me employed. You don't know how many cases I've won because of the nonsense people post on social media sites."

Unable to sit still, I get back up to refill my wine glass.

"Poor thing can't be any older than 25, just putting it all out there for everybody to see," she says, rambling on before stopping abruptly. Just as I turn to walk back to my seat, Taylor gasps and covers her mouth. "Dee, come look at this."

I approach Taylor and see an enlarged picture that is posted on Morgan's page that is a part of a collage she created, dated 30 weeks ago.

"Is that Jay's arm?" Taylor asks, pointing at the screen.

"You mean the one with this girl's name tattooed on it? Uh huh...looks like it! Oh and is that an engagement ring that she's bragging about?"

"Well, it looks like she's strolling down memory lane with this collage of photos, so at least it wasn't super recent," Taylor attempts to clarify.

"That may be true, but who lies about a baby? Then on top of that lies and says he's never been in love or in a serious relationship, yet your ex is all over social media with pictures of an engagement ring and her name tattooed on your body?"

Infuriated and in tears, I slam the laptop shut. "I don't want to see anymore."

In an effort to calm me down, Taylor stands up and guides me into the living room where she sits and holds me as I burry my face into her shoulder in tears. After nearly forty-five minutes of crying non-stop, I was done. I didn't have anything else left to give or another tear to shed. Instead of forcing me to talk about it, Taylor just held me and let me lay there in silence. We turn on the television to lighten the mood before falling asleep on the couch, side by side.

The next morning, I wipe the tear stained mascara lines from my face, feeling completely numb to everything that I found out the previous night. As if I can't escape him, I glance over at my phone to see six missed calls and several unopened text messages from Jay. Wanting all the drama to just disappear, I turn off my phone and close the window shades leaving the room pitch black before I slide into bed. Unable to drown out my thoughts completely, I force myself to sleep through the pain as I lay there crying myself to sleep in a puddle of my own tears all over again.

CHAPTER 13

After several days of moping around the house and calling out sick from work just to wallow in my own self-pity, Taylor and Gia decide it's time to cut my pity party short. They show up at my doorstep ready to pull me out of the funk I was in and help me to get back on track. I greet them at the front door wearing pajamas and a robe that I had slept in for the past two days, too depressed to get myself together. My bed was the only place I felt comfortable, so they followed me up the stairs and back into my bedroom.

"Damn, you should've told us we needed to bring backup!" Gia says with the look of disgust on her face, looking around my room as I climb back into bed.

"Ummm...we need to get Molly Maids on the line ASAP! This room is a disaster. I love you, Dee, but you know how I feel about manual labor. I'm not cleaning up this mess! Elijah's room is never this messy and he's still in elementary school!" Taylor adds with a look of disgust, clearing a section of clothes off of my bed before sitting down.

"Well, as you both can see, I haven't been in the mood to do much of anything lately."

"Mmm...Yeah, we noticed," Taylor mumbles, "But girl, that's what we're here for! You act like this is the first time a man has ever done you wrong! You got over Tate, didn't you? And another one came along shortly after, just like there will be another one after Jay!"

"Another what? Another fuck up with two...maybe three baby mamas this time? Another what, Taylor? Tell me!" I lose it. "I can't take anymore shit from another man! We're not 20 year old little girls with our entire lives ahead of us anymore, Tay! I'm a grown ass woman with a biological clock that is ticking and a mother who reminds me of it every five minutes. I'm tired of this cycle! I want a man whose word I don't have to question!"

Just the thought that maybe I would never get my happily ever after threw me back into a depression.

Gia reaches out to console me as I wipe away the tears streaming down my face. "Dulsey, I get it! I do. But shutting yourself off from the world and living in a bathrobe isn't going to make anything better. You can't run from your problems anymore!" Holding my shoulders, she looks up at me and says, "And that means facing Jay too. Before you write this man off, you should at least confront him and hear what he has to say. I'd just hate to see you give up on a relationship that has consistently kept a smile on your face these past few months."

"I agree with Gia on standing up to your problems," Taylor adds, "but I'm not for that jerk, Jay. I think you should take this as a loss and move on before you find yourself knee deep in some mess he created!"

"But she doesn't even know if it's his baby, Taylor! What if she prematurely gives up on a relationship that has a real chance over the word of some chick looking for a come up?"

"Gia, trust me! He's no good! You didn't see all the dirt we dug up on this fool the other day." She leans over and whispers to Gia, "I'll tell you about it in the car, girl."

"Guys, I don't think you're helping. I don't want to talk about Jay. I just want to sleep," I groan as I turn over and close my eyes.

Tugging at my pajamas, Taylor begins to get frustrated with my lack of interest in their conversation.

"You guys just don't get it. Y'all are so lucky. Even though you both had your own challenges in your relationships, at least you know what it feels like to be in love and you have your babies to remind you of that. But what do I have? Huh?" Sniffing and trying to hold back the tears, I feel myself start to break down again. "I just wonder if it's ever going to happen for me, or if I'm just being unrealistic with my expectations."

"Dee, now you know how crazy my relationship has been with my child's father and it definitely hasn't lived up to what I thought it would be! Love isn't a word I would ever use to describe us...stuck...yeah, that's more appropriate! I love my daughter so much, but I for sure wish I would've waited to start a family with the right man and that's why I admire you. You refuse to settle for less than you deserve instead of continuing to put years into a relationship that you know isn't healthy because it's comfortable or convenient," Gia confesses, looking up at the ceiling trying to prevent tears from falling.

"Stuck? Damn, what happened now? I thought y'all were working things out!" Taylor inquires.

"Yeah, me too until I ran across some text messages from some young girl he's been carrying on with." Stopping mid thought, Gia turns to look at me and says, "You know what? Get up and get out of those stank pajamas! We all need a drink!"

"Or two! Let's go!" Taylor echoes her sentiments, pulling the covers back from over me.

Before I know it, we're sitting at a high top table in the bar area of the closet restaurant we could find, ready to drown our relationship woes in a martini glass. Gia attempts to dodge questions about her relationship the entire car ride as if she had forgotten that she already let the cat out of the bag when we were back at my house. Therefore, it should be no surprise that it was the first topic of discussion as soon as we sat down. Gia should've known that Taylor wouldn't pass up this opportunity to ask her a million questions and get all in her business.

"So, what's going on with your man, Miss Gia?"

"Well, simply put...the mother fucker has lost his mind!" fuming, out of nowhere Gia's mood shifts dramatically as if she's reliving the hurt. "I just can't take his bullshit anymore!"

"I'm sorry, who are you and what have you done with my friend? Since when did mother fucker and bullshit become a part of your vocabulary?" I ask.

"Oh, I don't know where you got this new Gia from, but I like her!" Taylor says as she playfully high-fives Gia.

"Seriously, Gia. What's going on?" I question.

"Anthony came into town to spend some time with our daughter, and of course he was telling me that he wants to give us another shot so we can be a family. He was even telling me that he has an interview for a job in Arlington, so he can be closer to us. We've been in such a good space for the past year that I was starting to think he was really turning over a new leaf and could possibly be mature enough to handle us being a family again. Unfortunately, I was wrong. When he was taking a shower the other morning, his phone started to vibrate back to back like he was getting a ton of texts. I tried not to revert back to my old ways and start snooping, but my inner Taylor came out and I couldn't resist!"

"That's my girl!" Taylor adds.

"Of course his lock code is Elle's birthday, so once I got in I saw that he's been involved with this young girl that lives near him in Miami. The crazy part is, after my fishing expedition I was mad as hell for a little while but then I felt this strange calmness come over my body. I was ready to call this girl up and let her have it, but then I had to think about the man I was dealing with and how long he was able to string me along before I directed my anger at some innocent little girl. I mean, what good would it be to let all of my bottled up emotions go on a young girl who fell victim to the same lies and promises that I did. If it sounded good to me at 31, I'm sure it was music to her 20 something year old ears."

"This is sounding a bit like déjà vu! You've been with Anthony off and on for the better part of the last decade. And every time he pulls the same exact stunt, we sit here and we listen to you complain over and over again about the same thing. It's like a revolving door with you two, and I wish you could just stop and move on! I know you feel like since you put up with so many years of him dogging you out, that once he finally does straighten up..."

"If he ever straightens up," Taylor adds her two cents as I continue. "Exactly, if he ever straightens up, you feel like you should be the one to reap the benefits of it. I get it! But I also know you and how you will try to make a circle fit into a square peg when you know it doesn't fit! Just be thankful that you got Elle out of the whole ordeal, but it's time to let it go. I think we both need to let go! He is who he is and he only continues to sell you dreams because he knows you'll entertain his mess. Turns out Anthony and Jay have a lot in common."

"Okay, Dee! Remind me not to talk to you about my relationship when you're hurt! I need the nice, sweet Dulsey back! Sheesh!" Gia responds.

"But Gia, it's the truth and you need to hear it! You and Josey's ass! We should call her and put her on face time. She needs to hear it from Dee straight while she's in the mood to dish it out!" Taylor says.

"Taylor, shut up! That's not funny!" Gia takes offense.

"You and Josey trip me out! You both are always complaining about your situation, praying to God to deliver you from it, but when he does you run right back to these dogs and pray for them to change.

He's not gonna change, it's been eight years for God's sake! And in eight more years he's still gonna be a dog -- just an older, less attractive one. I love you and I want to be here for you, but I'm with Dulsey on this one. I'm tired of hearing you complain and it's not like I can help you because you're obviously okay with being treated this way because you keep going back and he knows it." Taylor pauses, looking around for a waiter before she picks up where she left off, "That's why he works you like a runway, honey. Walks all over your feelings turns, spins, reverses and does it all again, all while putting on a show for his boys as if his actions are admirable."

Trying not to come off as a negative Nancy, I try to redeem myself with Gia.

"I know you may not like what we have to say, and that's okay! I just want you to know that we'll never misguide you; never have, never will. We just know the extreme effect that Anthony tends to have on you and sitting back watching you turn into this angry, irrational woman that I can't connect with when you two are having issues is getting old. I want that happy-go-lucky Gia to stay! Not the 'I'm going through it with Anthony again' version of Gia."

"I agree! But speaking of..." Taylor clears her throat and directs her attention towards me, "We need our girlfriend back! And Gia, I don't know what your schedule looks like, but if we could have her back sometime this week, we'd greatly appreciate it!"

None of us could keep a straight face at that point. We all burst into laughter, hugging on one another.

Gia looks at us both, "I guess no matter how old we are, sometimes we like to take on a good project and feel like we can dress him up, inspire him, and teach him how to be a man. You win some, you lose some."

"Don't remind me! I'm 0-4 in this game of hearts. If I don't get a win soon, I may have to retire my losing record," I utter.

"On that note, grab that waiter! We need a drink. Now!" Taylor yells out, finally catching the waiter's attention.

CHAPTER 14

After being out until nearly two o'clock in the morning with the girls, I'm awakened by the sound of my house phone ringing non-stop. Barely able to remove my face from the fluffy pillows that it had been indented in all night, I pull the phone from the dock and press it to my ear. All I could hear was my mother's frantic voice, causing me to sit up straight in bed.

"Ma, calm down! What's going on?" I inquire, trying to get to the bottom of what's gotten her so worked up.

After a few moments, she finally formulates a coherent sentence. "It's your father! He was in a really bad car accident!"

"Oh my God! Is he okay?"

"I'm not sure, baby. They said it was really bad and they've transported him to the hospital. Please just try to get here as soon as you can! I'm going up to the hospital now to see what's going on."

"Okay, Ma! I'll check the flights and meet you there. Just keep me updated!"

"Of course I will, baby! I love you, travel safe," she says before hanging up.

Unsure of all of the emotions going through my body simultaneously, I try to stay positive as I book a flight leaving for Chicago within the next two hours. Rushing, I throw enough things into my suitcase to last a week and head to the airport.

I land half past noon to a voicemail from my mother letting me know my father's room number and that he's in stable condition. I couldn't help but feel relieved that my second chance with my father wasn't cut short. On the ride to the hospital, I promise myself that I will put forth a much bigger effort to be a part of his life and allow him to take on a bigger part in mine.

My mother greets me as I make my way towards his hospital room.

"Hey sweetie, I'm glad you made it!"

"Hey mom, how's he doing?"

"Oh, thank God he's much better!" she says sounding relieved.

"So what happened?"

"Well, he was driving to work this morning and had a heart attack. He lost control of his car and crashed into a tree. Thankfully, onlookers called for help immediately, otherwise the doctors say he could've died."

Unable to find words to respond, the severity of the situation started to kick in. The fact that I was so close to losing my father for good started to play on my conscience again. Interrupting my train of thought, my mother walks me to his room. She explains, "Now his wife and one of his daughters were here earlier, but they left to get him some things from home so you could have some alone time with him. I've been here all morning so I'm going to go on home now, but call if you need me."

I kiss my mother good-bye before pushing open the door to my father's hospital room to find him sitting up, wide awake watching television. Unsurprisingly, he was bruised up pretty badly, but seemed to be in good spirits.

"Hey Dad, how are you feeling?"

"Baby girl! I'm so glad you're here! You know I've had better days, but I'm not going to complain about it because I'm blessed to be alive."

"Indeed you are! Ma told me what happened! I'm just glad you're okay. So many things were going through my head when she called this morning."

Laughing, he responds, "You know Sharon has always been a worry wart! Poor woman had to deal with me, and I'm sure I 'bout worried her to death!"

We both giggled at the truth in his statement.

"I'm sorry...for everything. My attitude; how I acted. I know it's out of the blue, but I shouldn't have disrespected you like that," I blurt out, feeling like I couldn't hold it on my heart any longer.

"Baby girl, it's okay! You were hurt and I don't have much right to be offended because I played a huge part in causing that hurt. I'm just thankful that you finally came around!" he looks down at himself before continuing, "Well, I didn't plan to be in a hospital gown when you did, but you're here now and I couldn't be happier!"

I hug him gently before sitting at his bedside.

"So, Dulsey, tell me something. How are those boys treating you?" he asks.

Smiling to hide the hurt, I respond, "Okay, I guess." Shrugging off his question, he chuckles to himself at my response.

"What's so funny?" I ask.

"You just took me back to when you were a little girl, that's all! I would always have to ask you the same question at least three times before I got the truth out of you. I see you still haven't gotten enough of hiding your feelings!"

I shake my head with a smile at how accurate he is. "You're so right," I admit.

"So, how are those boys *really* treating my baby girl?"

"Oh, I hate them all!" I jokingly respond with a giggle, "I don't really hate them...that much! I just can't figure them out."

I felt the overwhelming urge to be completely honest and transparent with my father, so with my embarrassment aside, I explain to him in detail about my situation with Jay. He sits and listens intently as I speak without saying a word.

"So this Jay guy...do you think the baby is his? What do his actions tell you?" he asks.

"That's exactly the problem. He says there's a slim chance that he's the father, yet I found out through a friend of my girlfriend's that he's attending doctor's appointments and is apparently very involved with her pregnancy. Those just aren't the actions that come to mind when I think of someone who doesn't think there's a real chance that he's the father."

"Yeah, I agree. That's unusual behavior for someone who doesn't think that's his baby the young lady is carrying."

"And on top of that, Taylor, you know my lawyer friend who must've been an investigator in her past life, helped me dig up so much dirt on him after you warned me not to. I'm so torn. I want to believe that his feelings for me are genuine and that he wasn't just putting on a show for me with all those tears in the car, but when I see his ex posting recent pictures in his bed, it makes it hard for me to find him credible." I take a moment to reflect on my own words. "I just wish I could turn my heart off. It's stressing me out trying to find the one."

"Maybe that's the problem. You're trying too hard! When it's real, don't get me wrong, you have to work at it to maintain it but one thing you'll never have to do is force it. You never have to talk yourself into a good thing. That's a sign that it's anything but love, and let me tell you, that's what guys do! Dress up BS real nice and pass it off as love until they've gotten all that they want and use you up." Shaking his head and visibly upset, he continues, "Dulsey, he's using you. There's nothing about his character or actions that lets me know that he realizes how valuable you are. He doesn't know what he has because he's used to running through girls without a real emotional attachment. It's a vicious cycle that you've stumbled into and the moment you no longer benefit him, you get cut! You see, when a man wants you he looks at you as an investment. He's patient enough to build a solid foundation, to water the seed and enjoy being there to see it mature and grow. And after he's put in all of that work, you better believe he's going to stick around to reap the rewards.

When you rush into situations and give too much too soon, a man misses out on the opportunity to earn you. You can never give them too much! Never!"

I felt the weight of all of the truth in his words hit me all at once as the tears begin to flow.

"I'm sorry! Here I go again."

"Baby girl, you never have to apologize for your emotions!"

"I just never thought I'd be here. You know? I'm 32! Dad, seriously my eggs are shriveling up as we speak!" I say, laughing through my tears.

"Where did you get this timetable? Love is not on your watch! It comes when it feels good and damn ready. You should be happy it hasn't hit you yet..." he pauses abruptly.

"Why is that?" I lift my head and question out of confusion.

"Because you're not as ready as you think you are."

Feeling slighted, I stand up and look at him for a moment with a puzzled expression. "Robert, you've been back in my life for all of five minutes and already you think you've got me figured out?"

He motions towards me, "Come here. Sit back down! Let me explain."

"No...No," I utter as I calm myself in the corner of the room.

Quietly, Robert begins to speak, "I'm not ever going to be a man whose intentions you have to question. Whether you acknowledge it or not, you're mine! You're me! That's how I know you better than you know yourself!"

"I know," I admit, wiping my tears feeling like I was overreacting. "It's true...I'm sorry, I'm so embarrassed for reacting like this. This whole situation is hitting me way harder than I imagined." I look down at my watch, not realizing how much time had passed.

"I should go," I state as I walk over and kiss his forehead. "I'm gonna go check into my hotel. I'll be back in the morning to check on you."

"Okay, I'll see you in the morning then."

Finally arriving at my hotel, I decide to go up to my room and rest to reenergize myself which will hopefully pull me out of this weird mood that I've sunken into. As soon as I drop my bags and stretch out in the bed, my mother calls. We chat for a few minutes before I drift off to sleep shortly after hanging up.

Eight forty-seven; I'm awaken by the vibration of my cell phone. Feeling refreshed, I glance over at the clock before answering Josey's call, realizing that I had slept the day away.

"Hey Josey," I speak into the phone after answering.

"Hey Dee, how's your father doing?"

"Oh, girl he's doing a lot better. Thank God! Sorry I forgot to call you and the girls back to fill you in. I ended up coming straight to my hotel after I left the hospital and fell asleep as soon as I got in. I've literally been sleep all day!"

"No worries, Dee. We're just glad he's doing okay. I just wanted to run something by you, and then I'll let you get back to resting," Josey says.

"Okay, what is it?" I ask.

"I was wondering if you were free to come out to L.A. soon! I could really use some time with you girls, plus you haven't been out here to see my new place yet!" she pleads.

Thinking to myself for a moment, I respond, "You know what? That doesn't sound like a bad idea! I could really use a change of scenery to take my mind off of all the drama in my life right now."

"Great! Then it's settled! When can you come?"

"I'll have to double check my schedule, but I'm pretty sure I have a few days off after my work trip on Thursday. I should be able to fly out Friday morning and stay through the weekend. I'll talk to the girls and see if they're free that weekend too."

"Okay, sounds great! I'll see you soon."

"Okay, bye."

I hang up the phone, envisioning how nice it will feel to be surrounded by warm weather and sunshine as I gaze at the pouring rain outside. In need of a drink and a bite to eat, I head downstairs to the bar area when I notice a familiar face. It was Kenny, the flirtatious bartender that had the bad boy thing going on from my last visit to Chicago. As I approach the bar, he looks over and smiles letting me know that he hasn't forgotten me either.

"You look phenomenal!" he says, staring at me with a grin.

"Really?" I respond, stunned, "Well, thanks! Not bad for sitting in a hospital room and sleeping most of the day, I guess."

"Awww, man! Is everything okay?" he says with a look of genuine concern.

"Oh, yeah. Well, it is now. My dad had a heart attack, but he's doing much better."

"Glad to hear he's doing okay! I was wondering what brought you all the way back to the Windy City." He looks away for a moment, before continuing, "I was feeling myself for a minute though, I must admit."

"And why is that?" I question.

"I was kind of hoping you had come back to see me, you know!" he says throwing his hands up as if he was a prize. "A man can dream, can't he?"

Laughing probably a little too hard, I respond, "Oh, yeah? You were definitely feeling yourself! You may be cute, but that's a long trip to take just to watch you pour a couple drinks!"

Raising his eyebrows, he blurts out, "Ah huh! So you think I'm cute? See, now we're getting somewhere!"

I shrug in laughter at his flirtation.

"Hold that thought!" He then walks over to tend to a couple seated at the opposite end of the bar. I remembered that I needed to text Taylor and Gia back to update them on my father's condition, so I fiddle for my phone in my purse only to find a few missed calls from Jay. Just seeing his name displayed in my phone made me think about all the pictures posted by his ex and all of his hurtful lies that pushed me over the edge emotionally. Just as I began to fall back into my feelings, his name illuminates on my cell phone screen once more. Without thinking of what I would say, I finally answer his call after trying so hard to erase his existence from my memory.

"What do you want, Jay?"

"Dulsey, I'm glad you answered! I've been calling and texting you like crazy all week long."

"I noticed," I say with as little emotion as possible.

"Can we meet up and talk about this face to face? This whole situation is just crazy and it's gotten out of hand! I need to see you so I can make this right!"

"You can't un-do her pregnancy, so how do you intend to make this situation right?"

"I know that. This isn't the most ideal situation, I understand. But you also have to know that I just don't want to be portrayed as that fucked up guy in the unlikely event that it is my child! Listen, just let me see you face to face. I will answer any and every question you have! I'm going to make this right! Please!"

"No."

"Please, hear me out! Just this once, I promise I can make this right."

"Jay, what more is there to say? You lie when you don't have to and you cheat, and then do a poor job of covering your tracks on top of everything. It's hard to trust you when I've given you every opportunity to tell the truth and you choose to lie instead. And your temper is an issue for me. I'm scared that one day you'll direct your aggression towards me."

"I know, and you're right. I know I have to work to keep my temper in check and stop shutting down when things get tough. But I've never once lost my temper with you! I only get like that because of all my family drama and all of the other chaotic shit on my plate, but you're the only thing that keeps me sane. I admit, it was wrong not to tell you about the possibility of me becoming a father, but everything else was all me! I know I've lost your trust, but know that everything else that I told you was real and I'm willing to do whatever it takes to gain your trust back."

"Really?" I question.

"Yes, Dulsey!"

"So you're telling me everything else you told me about yourself was true, right?"

"Every word."

"You do realize omitting the truth and telling a bold face lie is essentially the same thing, don't you?"

"I understand that. Where are you going with this?"

Blindsiding him, I ask, "Whose name is tattooed on your arm?"

"What are you talking about? I have a lot of tattoos."

"Any of them your ex-fiancée's name?"

My outburst is met with silence. He sighs loudly after a few moments, knowing he was caught in yet another lie. "That's a long story and it's not what you think," he attempts to explain.

"What I think is everything that comes out of your mouth is questionable. I feel like I don't even know you."

He fell silent once again as I look over my shoulder at Kenny making drinks at the other end of the bar. Regaining my attention, Jay finally responds, "I know that I have been an imperfect man but all that aside, I need you! I can't take you walking out of my life right now."

Wanting to end this conversation, I state, "I need some time to think things through. If I feel up to meeting with you, then I'll be in touch. If not, please just let me be."

Sounding reluctant, "Okay. That's fair. I really hope I see your beautiful face soon. I love you," he responds.

"Yeah, hopefully," I say as I end the call.

I walk back to my seat at the bar and finish off the last bit wine resting at the bottom of my glass. The lonely feeling of emptiness creeps up on me again as I watch the couple at the other end of the bar interacting. He is so into her and can barely keep his hands off of her. I envied them in that moment. I miss feeling like I mattered to a man. Just watching that couple brought back such intense memories of how Jay was with me. The chemistry we shared gave me so much hope because I hadn't felt loved in such a long time, nor had I ever felt loved on such an intense level before. The first week that we met, we were literally inseparable. I still consider it to be one of the best weeks of my life by far. I felt awakened on the inside and so alive just being in his presence. We truly brought out the best in each other as we spent our days talking about the future, laughing, or playing around every chance we got. I wanted to feel all those things instead of feeling like I've failed at love once again. I just didn't want the bad that followed, like seeing him lose his temper or finding out that he's a cheater. I don't want to be the only person in this relationship in love.

Waving Kenny over, I decide that I need to do something to get my mind off of all of Jay's drama. I yell out as he approaches, "I need a shot! And so do you!"

"My kind of lady!" Kenny says, obliging my request. He brings over two tequila shots with a smile. "So what shall we cheers to?"

"How about...to living in the moment for once!" I propose.

"I like how that sounds!" Kenny says.

We clink our shot glasses and down the tequila in one gulp. Unable to keep my cool, the strength of the alcohol overcomes me and leaves me with the worst sour face known to man. It wasn't cute, but Kenny seemed to be getting a kick out of it!

Once I was finally able to recover, I look over at Kenny to find him staring at me intently which caught me a little off guard.

"It's getting late, I think I'm gonna get ready to head upstairs," I say to Kenny.

"I enjoyed your company tonight...a lot. I hope I get to see you again before you leave," he says.

I nod my head and turn to walk away as he stands there with his hands planted firmly on the bar. I stop dead in my tracks at the thought of going back to an empty hotel room and turn around to see Kenny still standing there watching me walk away.

"So, what time do you get off?" I bluntly ask.

He pauses for a moment, smiling, and then looks down at his watch. "In about forty-five minutes. Why?" he asks, side eying me.

I glance down at my feet trying to garner up the confidence to say what I really truly wanted. Against my better judgment, I finally respond, "Well...if you're not doing anything after work...I was thinking maybe you can come by my room for a night cap."

Unable to read his facial expression, I blurt out regretfully, "I'm sorry for being so forward. I just don't want to be alone tonight." Nervously fidgeting, I quickly turn to walk away yelling over my shoulder "Forget I said anything!"

"Wait Dulsey! Don't worry, you won't be alone tonight. I'll bring up a bottle of wine when I'm done here," he winks, then smiles emphasizing his gorgeous dimples.

Unable to tame my smile, I turn and respond, "Okay, I'm in 803."

"Don't fall asleep on me!" he jokes as I walk towards the elevator with a little extra pep in my step.

Ten thirty rolls around, and by this time I'm lounging across the bed in a hotel robe, fresh out of the shower. Eager for Kenny's arrival, I turn on some music to set the mood when Janet Jackson's 'Again' comes blaring through the speakers.

"Oh, no! Wrong song!" I mumble under my breath. Just listening to that song reminds me of Jay and makes me want to give into my heart instead of my head. He should be the furthest thing from my mind at this point. After several minutes of shuffling through music selections, I give up and toss the phone on the bed. Every note of every song brings me back to the moments I shared with Jay. So silence it is. I'll just let Kenny be the entertainment tonight instead.

Chapter 15

Just as I start to get lost in thought lying on the bed and staring at the ceiling, I hear a knock at the door. I spring up, adjusting myself to make sure that not one hair is out of place before I open the door to find Kenny standing there with a grin.

"Still up for that drink?" he asks as he holds up two bottles of merlot.

"Two bottles, huh! You're not trying to get me drunk and take advantage of me are you?"

Laughing, he responds, "Me? Never!" Smiling, I nod and gesture for him to come in. He walks in and sets the bottles of wine on the marble counter top above to mini bar. He turns around and gazes into my eyes before continuing his thought, "Besides, I would want to make sure you remembered every moment."

"Oh, is that right?" I question, intrigued by his response.

He walks up to me from behind, moving the hair from my neck before kissing it slowly. The warmth from his touch and each sensual kiss on my neck gave me such a high. I turn to face him and kiss him passionately as his hands begin to venture up my thigh. The passion we share begins to climax as I tear open his black collared shirt while he unties my robe, pulling it down my arms and dropping it to the floor. Pressed against one another, he forces me down to the bed where he lays in between my legs and caresses my thighs, kissing me gently.

Just as he starts to slowly kiss me from my mouth down to my waist, the reality of my actions start to set in. This isn't me. I barely know Kenny. And even though his touch feels like the answer to my loneliness, in the back of my mind I know that I'll regret this in the morning.

"Ugh, why couldn't I wait to have a conscience in the morning?" I mutter under my breath before stopping Kenny mid kiss.

"What's wrong, babe?" he asks.

"I'm so sorry, Kenny. I just can't do this. I thought I was ready, but something just doesn't feel right!" I admit.

Puzzled, he sits up beside me on the edge of the bed.

"Okay. So, do you want me to leave?"

Trying to avoid making this situation any more awkward than it already is, I turn to him and smile, "We still have two unopened bottles of merlot to drink first. I enjoy your company, and I could really use some tonight." Staring at him wishing I knew what he was thinking, I ask, "So what do you say?" I get up and pour two glasses of wine and offer one to him.

"Can't let this good wine and good company go to waste! Of course I'll stay," he responds as he accepts the glass from me.

"Thank you."

Truth is I felt guilty as Kenny attempted to make love to me because all I could think about was Jay and how much I wish that it was his hands caressing me instead. Thankfully Kenny was understanding of my fragile state and stayed up all night drinking wine, cuddling, and watching Beaches with me.

The next morning I wake up to find myself in bed...alone. I sit up, draw the covers back and notice a message scribbled on the notepad by the side table. Apparently Kenny slipped out last night after I fell asleep because he had to tend to some "early morning errands". I'm sure that was code for "I had to escape while I could to avoid that awkward conversation in the morning", and for that I'm even more grateful to him. I had no clue what I would say if I woke up next to him after the wine and lonely late night feeling had worn off.

After I finish showering I turn on the television to catch the end of the morning news. As I pour myself a cup of coffee, the phone rings. A local phone number pops up on my cell phone belonging to the hospital. I answer to find my father on the other end.

"Hey Dulsey, I have some very special people here that I'd like you to meet. What time do you plan to come back to the hospital?" Robert asks.

"Okay! I can throw on some clothes and be there within the hour."

"Wonderful! I'll see you soon!" he says with such excitement.

I hang up and proceed to get ready. As I pull on my rugged denim jeans and wrestle through my suitcase to find a sweater to pull on, I decide to dial up my mom and touch base with her.

"Hey baby," she answers on the first ring.

"Hey Ma, what are you up to?"

"Oh, not much! Just about to make some tea and finish reading this book for my book club meeting this weekend."

"Okay, I won't bother you then. I just wanted to see if you were going back up to the hospital, but I think I got my answer."

"Robert has you, his wife and other children there to check on him. I'm sure you all will keep him company. It'll actually be a great time to meet your half siblings and his new wife. I met his wife, Yvonne, briefly yesterday and she seems like a nice lady. She don't take no mess, but she's real classy with it. I'm not mad at her," she says.

"Ma, turn off MTV and BET and stick to Lifetime please. I don't know when you started talking like this, but I can't take it!" I say, laughing at my mother's new colloquialism.

"Dee, chill!" she adds in jest.

"Good-bye mother! You are just too much today!"

She giggles and then responds, "Bye baby! Or should I say peace out! That's what the young kids are saying now, right?"

Shaking my head at her silliness, "Sorry Ma, you're about two decades too late with that one. Nice try though!"

Chapter 16

"Hey dad!" I exclaim as I walk into his hospital room and greet him with a hug.

"Hey there, baby girl! I'm so glad you made it!" he says, hugging me firmly. "I have some special ladies that I can't wait for you to meet! They should be back from the cafeteria in a few minutes, but until then have a seat and talk to your old man!"

"I'm excited to meet them! I just wish Cory could be here to meet his sisters too," I say somberly.

"I know, Dulsey. I wish your brother was here too. But he'll be done with his tour soon, so we have to stay positive and focus on all the great things waiting on him when he gets home."

"You're right! I can't wait to write to him over in Afghanistan and tell him about everything that's been going on! He's overdue for a care package anyway, so I need to stop and get some Garrett's popcorn!

I'm sure you remember how much he loved that popcorn as a kid!"

"I sure do!" he says with a reminiscent tone, just as his doctor walks in.

"How are you doing, Mr. Davenport?" he inquires.

"Feeling much better, doc!" my father answers.

"Well, I've got some good news. All the tests are looking good so far, so it looks like you'll be out of here the day after tomorrow at the latest."

"Alright, doc. Thank you."

As the doctor exits the room, a woman walks in with brunette hair flowing down her back. She was a heavy set woman, but she carried it well. She had the presence of a woman who didn't tolerate any mess, so immediately I knew this had to be my father's new wife, Yvonne. Her presence alone demanded respect and I appreciated that. I don't know why I was expecting a push over or a puppet, but this further reassures me that my father really has gotten his act together and that she must have had a hand in that.

"You must be Dulsey! I've heard so much about you!" she says extending her hand out to me. "I'm Yvonne, Robert's wife."

Accepting her hand and shaking it softly, I reply, "It's so nice to meet you!"

"I had the pleasure of meeting your mother yesterday. She's a fine woman, and I'm sure you are equally amazing."

"I talked to my mom this morning and she had nothing but nice things to say about you as well."

She walks over to my father and adjusts his pillow and helps him get more comfortable before sitting next to him on the bed. "Your dad is a much better man now," she states, gazing over at him with a smile. "The man your mom married certainly isn't the same man laid up here in this hospital bed today. Bless her heart for dealing with this knucklehead as long as she did," she jokingly adds with a smile, nudging him gently. "We're all on a journey and he's had his share of pitfalls; some by his own wrong doing. He may have learned what it takes to be a man late in life, but I'm fortunate that he got the memo some men live their whole lives without ever getting."

I chime in, "I completely agree."

"Sometimes it takes getting to know a man's past to understand the man in front of you and I'm glad you have opened up your heart to Robert again and allowed him the opportunity to get to know you as a woman and for you to get to know a better version of him. That takes strength and a forgiving heart!"

"It's definitely been a process, but having Robert back in my life is helping me heal old wounds and break bad habits in my own personal relationships. His words have been helpful thus far and I really do look forward to rebuilding our relationship. I really need that right now."

She smiles for a moment as she looks over at my father, then turns to me, "Dulsey, why don't you come walk with me to the vending machines. The girls are bringing the food but I forgot to get the drinks and I could use an extra hand."

"Sure," I say in agreement as I follow her out of the room. As soon as we're in the hallway, I turn to question Yvonne out of sheer curiosity, "So what's the secret?"

She laughs nervously. "What secret?" seeming slightly confused by my question.

"You know! With my father! I need a step by step guide on how to make men grow up and be responsible in every aspect of their lives. From the looks of things, you've done a pretty good job with my father!"

"Oh, I can't take all the credit for that even though I would like to, because you can't make a man do anything he isn't ready to do on his own," she says with a giggle. "In my experience anyway, that's just not how things work with men. You can see the potential and want more for them all day long, but if they don't want it for themselves, it's pointless." We continue to walk through the hospital hallway passing the nurse's station before Yvonne continues. "Your father put me through some stressful years initially, so I don't want you to get the impression that it's been a cake walk for me and that I snapped my fingers and made him be a better man." She pauses for a moment to clear her throat as we reach the vending area, "The first year your father and I got together, he conceived Riley with another woman. I was beyond devastated, but...I stayed."

"Oh my goodness, I'm sorry. I never knew that."

"It was difficult for me to endure, but at that time I was afraid of being alone and I didn't want to give up on your father and all the time I invested in our relationship. So some time passed and then a couple years later I got pregnant with Summer. As naive as I was, I thought that would make him want to be a better man and want to settle down, but he still wasn't ready."

"So what changed? Obviously he got the memo at some point, right?" I eagerly question.

"Well, when I was a few months pregnant he had a pregnancy scare with another woman and I found out. That was my breaking point. Between his cheating and continually falling off the wagon with his drinking problem, I finally chose me and the life of my unborn child over his foolishness and I left."

"I'm sure that got his attention."

"You would think!" she responds, shaking her head. "But his downward spiral continued until he hit rock bottom. By that time, Summer was five. He finally came to me, humbled with a genuine heart asking if I could help him get back on track. He started going to AA meetings routinely and became an excellent father after being in and out of the girls' lives for so long. Then two years into his sobriety and rebuilding his life, he asked me to marry him and I've yet to feel a moment of regret since accepting his proposal all those years ago."

"Wow, that's quite a story. I think I'm struggling with something similar," I admit.

"With Jay, right? That's his name?"

"Yeah, Jay."

"Your father mentioned him yesterday. I think he feels like his bad karma is rubbing off on you!"

"I knew he was to blame," I say jokingly. "No, I'm afraid this is all my own doing. Well, sort of. It didn't help that Jay wasn't honest and upfront with me, but I allowed things to move way too fast. So now I don't know what to do. I struggle between being patient and waiting this thing out to see if he lives up to the man he claims to be, or just walking away now while I still have a little dignity left."

"That's a tough one!" she says, bending down to get the last of the sodas out of the vending machine. "But I will say this, be careful who you let in your heart because once they're in there, it's hard as hell to get them out."

"Tell me about it! I think I may have already crossed that point of no return."

"It's never too late, but the longer you wait and the more time you invest, the harder it will be to walk away. You have to ask yourself if he's worth that risk and be prepared to be disappointed if he doesn't live up to what you need him to be."

"That's the thing. I see so much better for him because he is a good guy, but he's on the brink of being great and I feel like I can help bring that out of him," I explain.

"I understand, but my advice is to be careful. If a man isn't ready, you can't force him. He'll either end up resenting you or you'll end up with a failed relationship when it's not thoughtfully entered into voluntarily by both parties. And by ready, I don't mean based solely on his words or promises to be better because men have mastered the art of deceit and slick talking. I mean his actions, because his actions will either follow through or fall short and that's what you should base your decision off of. You have to get out of your heart and use your head on this one or else you have a lot of heartache waiting for you."

As we head back to my father's room, I fall silent internalizing

Yvonne's words and thinking about what the future holds for my relationship with Jay — if there even is one. After a few moments I turn to Yvonne, "Thank you! I really appreciate this talk and getting your perspective on things."

"Oh, it's no problem," she says, throwing her arm around me and pulling me close.

We walk back into the room and set the drinks down on the table beside my father's bed.

"I thought you ladies got lost, you were gone so long!" he says grinning at us.

"No, we just had a little girl talk. That's all!"

Just as I finish speaking, two girls walk into the room holding several bags of food.

"Dulsey! These are your sisters, Summer and Riley," Robert says.

The girls both greet me and give me hugs before sitting down and pulling their chairs closer to mine. They brought back enough food from the cafeteria to feed a small village, so we all dug in, eating and talking for the next few hours.

I spent the next two days by my father's side as he recovered and my new extended family was right there with me. It turned into a Cliff's Notes version of everyone's life stories compiled, to bring each of us up to speed regarding one another. Summer told me about all the sports she's involved in and how she's looking forward to getting her driver's license in the coming months. Riley told me about her college prep classes and how she wants to come visit me so I can take her to tour Georgetown's campus. I in turn told them about my career in aviation and about all of the amazing places I have been. I also told them as much as I could about our brother, Cory, who's halfway through his tour in Afghanistan. I couldn't wait to tell him all about his new family, as I'm sure it would be a welcomed distraction.

After leaving the hospital on the last day of my father's stay, I realize that leaving Chicago felt completely different than it ever had before. This time I felt more hopeful about my life and my family. I was actually looking forward to the next chapter with all of these new characters to get my mind off of a few of the old ones that I would have to face upon my return home.

CHAPTER 17

It was nearly nine o'clock in the evening when I finally returned to my hotel after my father was cleared to leave the hospital. Once he was discharged, I decided to see him home and spend a few more hours with him before I fly out early the next morning.

Though I was exhausted from the day's events, I decide to pack my suitcase in preparation for my flight when I hear a knock at the door. Puzzled, I tip toe to the door and peek through the peep hole to find Kenny fidgeting outside of my door. After a few moments, I open the door, "Hey, I wasn't expecting to see you!"

"Hey Dulsey, I overheard you telling the front desk that tonight will be your last night. I just wanted to see you before you leave to at least give you a proper good-bye, face to face."

"That's sweet of you. You can come in for a few if you'd like," motioning him into my room.

"Sure, that'd be great," he responds.

As he swiftly walks in, the smell of his cologne catches my attention. I was slightly both surprised and intrigued. I wasn't expecting him to be wearing such a bold, mature scent. He sits and stares at me from the edge of the bed, looking at me like he had intentions that went far beyond a mere good-bye. The look in his eyes made me wonder if he wanted to leave a more lasting impression.

"I can't believe you're leaving me again! When's the next time you plan to visit."

"Well, I'm not sure. I don't have anything in the works right now," I lie, knowing I had already promised my sisters and Robert that I would be back next month. I was afraid to commit to seeing him the next time I come back. Starting something with Kenny would be dangerous for me, especially since I've yet to work out my feelings for Jay. I didn't want to lead him on, so I figured it would be easier this way.

Seeming a little frustrated, he responds, "Well maybe I can come see you! I have family in D.C.!"

Curve ball! Caught off guard, I turn my back to him and peer out of the window as I nervously think of a response. "Ummm...okay," I reply, secretly hoping he was just talking and had no real intentions of coming.

I turn to face him before staring down at my watch, hoping he would take the hint.

"Oh, I'm sorry! I know it's getting late and you're probably leaving really early in the morning, huh?"

"Yeah, 6 a.m.!" I respond.

"Okay, well can I get a hug before I leave since I have no idea when I'll see you again?"

I smile, nodding my head as I walk over to the edge of the bed where he's now standing.

He begins to hug me tightly as I exhale into his arms and close my eyes. It feels good to be in the arms of someone who hugs you as if they never want to let go. I feel him kiss the top of my forehead as I slowly look up at him and gently kiss his lips. Maybe I will let him make this a good-bye to remember after all.

CHAPTER 18

"Hey Taylor!"

"Hey Dee, thanks for finally returning a phone call! I was starting to get nervous."

"I know. I'm sorry. I spent a lot of time at the hospital with my dad and my sisters."

"Oh, great! How's he doing?" she asks.

"Much better! He's home now, resting. I think this whole accident was a blessing in disguise. Being out there allowed me to meet my other siblings and Robert's wife, who is a really nice woman. I got a chance to leave my problems in D.C. for a little while and get back to feeling like myself again."

"That's good to hear. You definitely needed a break from the drama, girl!"

"Yeah. I got that and so much more..." I respond, thinking of how great my last night in Chicago turned out.

"I'm sorry, is there a part of this story I missed?" Taylor questions.

"Well..." I hesitate for a moment, "Maybe a little part that I sort of skipped over by accident."

"By accident, huh?" she laughs, "Nice try, but as your best friend you are required to tell me all of your juicy secrets! And it sounds to me that you have added to that arsenal of juiciness and neglected to tell me all about it! Spill it!" Taylor demands.

"Okay, okay!" laughing, I continue, "I saw Kenny, the bartender from my last visit again and we talked...and maybe hung out a little."

"What are we, in the eighth grade? You hung out? That's all?"

"Well, no. But at first, yeah. The first night I was there I got a little tipsy trying to get my mind off of Jay and sort of invited him up to my room for a night cap."

"Now we're talking!" Taylor interjects.

"But we didn't do anything. We just cuddled, drank wine, and watched Beaches."

"Don't tell me you made that poor boy suffer through two hours of the ultimate chick flick without any action!" she says, jokingly.

"I did, actually! And Beaches is a great movie, so hush!"

"Okay, you're right. So you guys just laid there all night? With your clothes on? Boring! I hope this story gets better, but continue."

"Yeah, that was pretty much it. We tried to take it there but all I could think about was Jay, so I stopped him and the next morning I woke up to find that he had left after I fell asleep. I thought that was it, but then my last night in Chicago he pops up at my room...and well, the next thing I know we were butt naked on the floor!"

"On the floor?" she exclaims.

"Well, yeah. The floor...the couch...the bed...girl, everywhere!" I admit.

"Everywhere?"

"Yes, Taylor. Everywhere!" I dramatically reiterate.

"Yeah, yeah, I get it! So y'all were just having wild rabbit sex everywhere!"

"Girl, you have no idea! My back still hurts!"

"See girl, now that's your problem!"

"What?" I ask, confused.

"You're just giving it away! These men don't know what it feels like to earn a good woman. You're making it too easy!"

"Really, Taylor? Are you really giving me this lecture right now?" I sarcastically reply.

"Yes, Dee, really! Does your job just cut you a check every two weeks for fun or do you have to take your ass in there every week and earn it?"

"Point taken, but it's not like I wanted anything more from him. For heaven's sake, he's in Chicago and I'll probably never see him again."

"Yeah right! Until the next time you go home to see your parents! Stop playing."

"Well, maybe I'll stay somewhere new for once," trying to sound convincing, knowing I was lying through my teeth.

"Yeah, yeah! Sure you will. But on a serious note, we have to stop complaining about guys who just want one thing when you're out here playing the same games."

"Speaking of games..." I pause for a moment looking down at my phone, "I have the king of them beeping in on my other line."

"Who? Jay?"

"You know it!"

"Mmm...I saw him play on Sunday. You better tell him to get back on his game because baby mamas are expensive these days!"

After laughing at her bluntness, we agree to catch up further tomorrow before I click over to take Jay's call. Against my better judgment, we talk for a few minutes and I eventually give in to his request to meet up. I still needed to regroup from my trip and get some rest and he was just arriving home from an away game, so we agreed to meet up later that night at my house.

———

Seven o'clock rolls around a lot quicker than I had hoped. I was still reeling from the last few days and could use another hour or two of rest. I lazily pull myself together and force myself to get ready, even though I would much rather lay in bed than wait for Jay to come over and have this dreaded conversation. But I guess it is time to stop running from the situation since I can't avoid it forever. I made sure to be well put together, but not too over the top. I threw on a denim snap-front collared shirt with a tan, fitted pencil skirt that hugs my curves to remind him of what he's been missing. And I was sure to spray on a bit of the Gucci Guilty perfume that I know he likes to tantalize his senses.

Just as I pull out two wine glasses, I see the reflection of his headlights through the living room window. I pull out a bottle of merlot from the wine rack and set it down on the wooden coffee table next to the glasses before I open the door. As soon as the door swings open, Jay is standing there with a dozen long stemmed red roses.

"Hey Dulsey, I brought these for you," he says, extending the flowers towards me.

"Thank you, they're beautiful."

I invite him in and we sit down on my ivory leather sofa for a moment before I offer him a glass of wine.

"You look great by the way," he adds, staring at me squarely in the eye.

"Thanks."

"So how have you been? It's been so long since I've laid eyes on you."

"I've been maintaining. Had a few family matters to tend to which has been keeping me busy."

"Is everything okay?" he asks.

"Yeah, everything is good with my family now. My personal life, on the other hand, could use some work," I say with a tinge of sarcasm in my voice.

"I know, and that's why I'm here. First, I just want you to know how much I truly care about you. You don't know what a breath of fresh air you've been in my life. With all the drama going on around me from work to the possibility of being a dad, you were the only thing keeping me sane." He pauses for a moment, taking a deep breath before continuing, "I know what I did was wrong. I should've told you from the beginning that I may have gotten another woman pregnant and you shouldn't have had to find that out from anyone but me. It's just that I didn't expect to fall for you so fast and when I did, I was scared that if I told you too soon, you would leave."

"What made you think that? We're not exactly spring chickens! Most people our age have children these days. Of course in a perfect world I would like to be the only woman to bear your children, but if that's not the case, I have the right to know upfront."

"I didn't expect for things to go so fast with us. It's like we met and went on our first date one minute and the next minute, we're in love. I just got so caught up that I could never find the right time to bring it up."

"But after getting to know me, it bothers me that you felt like I wouldn't understand or that I would just walk away. I can't fault you for a decision that you made before we met, but I can place blame when you purposely deceive me."

"I understand."

"Do you really? Because I don't think you realize how much damage your lying has really caused. Everything that we've built has been on a lie and that makes it very difficult to trust you again!"

After a few moments of silence, I could tell he was at a loss for words. But I still had more questions brewing.

"So do you want to be with her?" I ask, unsure of if I could actually handle the response.

"It's difficult, because I want to be the father that I never had. I never imagined myself in this situation! It was supposed to be nothing more than a fling, so now I'm wrestling with what the right thing to do is. I'm not in love with her and I don't have any romantic feelings for her, but I'm afraid that she will be the type to withhold my child from me if the two of us aren't in a good space." Taking a moment, seemingly wrestling with his own thoughts, "I can't believe that I could possibly be having a baby with a woman that I don't even like, let alone love. It's all too much on me right now."

"Yeah...tell me about it," I grumble under my breath.

"I'm sorry. I don't think I have a clear answer. I'm still trying to figure this whole thing out myself, but I still want to be with you, as confusing as that sounds."

"And I want you too...but I don't want this..." I struggle to find the words to describe all of his excess baggage.

"I know," he says in a low tone, looking down at his feet.

With two full glasses of untouched wine on the table, the conversation and the awkward silences grew longer and more frequent. Thinking back to our first date, I would've never imagined that we would be here.

"I'm just so sorry. I don't know what to say. I should've never dragged you into my mess by letting things go farther than friends until I knew the outcome of this situation. Now things are just so complicated."

"Yeah. It's a little too late for that now. All we can do at this point is see how things turn out. Until then, I think it's best that we just remain friends— very distant ones."

"Wow! I knew that would be your response, but I'll do my best to respect it." He presses his hands against his knees and stands up, "I guess I'll be on my way then."

He walks towards me with his arms open to embrace me, so I reciprocate and hug him without getting too close.

"Damn, you smell so good," he says, as I smile to myself.

Jay places his hand under my chin and pulls my lips to his before kissing me with such passion. He pulls himself away as if his heart and mind were at war before ripping open my denim blouse, exposing my black lace bra underneath. Caught by surprise, yet still strongly attracted to him, I began to wrestle with my own heart. Before I can process all that's happening, he pulls my skirt up and bends me over the edge of my sofa. Trying to justify this moment to myself in my head as our final good-bye, he thrust himself inside of me continuously as I brace myself against the couch, barely able to grip the leather with my fingertips.

I turn to face him and stare directly into his eyes, as he pulls me into his chest. He hugs me so tight that I almost lose my breath then whispers calmly, "I'm sorry, but I can't let you go."

Those words calmed my heart, but as soon as I left the warmth of his embrace the severity of the situation was still weighing heavily on me. Jay fell onto the couch, pulling me down with him as we lay there in silence holding each other throughout the night without uttering a single word. We both kept holding on...even though we knew it was time to let go.

Chapter 19

My phone rings, abruptly waking me up from a deep sleep. I sit up straight, wiping my eyes to notice Jay was still laying by my side, unbothered. I reach for my phone and answer it quickly before it wakes him up too.

"Hello?" I whisper into the phone as I tip toe into the kitchen.

"Hey Dulsey!"

"Josey? Girl, it's eight o'clock in the morning here so that means it's five in L.A. Why in the hell are you up so early?" I question.

"I haven't been sleeping well the past few weeks, so I've been having a lot of late nights and early mornings."

"Is everything okay?"

"Well, that's why I called. I'm in need of some girl time, like ASAP! Did you talk to the girls about coming out here?"

"Oh, yeah. Taylor is working on a big case, so she won't be able to get away and Gia doesn't have anyone to watch Elle. I'm leaving for a work trip tomorrow, but when I get back I can come see you for a few days like we talked about before. How does that sound?"

"Sounds perfect, even though I wish the whole crew could come."

"Yeah, me too. I'm about to go back to sleep, but I'll text you the dates and my flight info later on."

"Great, can't wait to see you! Sorry to interrupt your sleep, get some rest."

I hang up and switch my phone to silent as I walk back into the living room. By this time Jay is wide awake, putting his shoes on.

"Ahhh, where'd you sneak off to?" he asks as he stands up to buckle his belt properly.

"I didn't want to wake you, so I went into the kitchen to take Josey's call."

"I thought I might've been keeping you from someone," he says with a side smirk.

"Right, like you're in any position to speak if there really was someone else in the picture."

"Ouch! That's cold!" he responds, wrapping his arms around me and kissing my cheek softly. "I have to go to practice, but I want to see you tonight. Okay?"

"Okay."

I walk him to the door and watch him get into his car and drive away, more confused now than when he came. Though my words set the stage for this to be the final chapter, my actions opened the door for this cycle to continue. Feeling more lost than ever, I pull my laptop from the desk and plop back onto the couch to search for flights out to L. A. I need to get away and clear my mind.

———

Later on that afternoon I get a call from Jay asking me to come over for dinner. This man can barely cook eggs without following a recipe, so I figured he really meant take out.

Just as I finished packing an overnight bag, I hear my phone ringing in the kitchen. I race down the stairs to see that it's Jay calling. I answer quickly, hoping to catch him before he hangs up.

"Hey!"

"Hey babe, you sound out of breath!"

"I am. I just ran down the stairs to answer the phone!"

"So, yeah babe, remind me to get you a gym membership! Your four whole steps should not have you out of breath!" he says laughing to himself, never missing an opportunity to tell a joke.

"Ha ha, very funny!" mocking him, "I'm on my way now."

"That's actually why I'm calling. My driver just picked me up from practice. Since we finished up a little early, I'm headed into the city. I figured I would swing by and get you, then we can pick up dinner and head back to my place."

"Okay, that works!"

"Cool. We're about fifteen minutes away."

"Okay, see you then."

Fifteen minutes to the tee, his black Cadillac Escalade pulls up in front of my brownstone. I grab my keys from the mahogany side table and pick up my black, leather duffle bag and exit the front door. Jay's driver walks around and opens the back passenger side door for me as I climb in and greet Jay with a kiss.

"Hey babe, so where are we going for dinner?" I ask.

"I thought I would take you to this little carryout in Northeast D.C. near my grandma's house where I grew up. I know it's not anything fancy like where we usually go, but it's one of my favorites."

"That's okay! I'm down to try something different!"

"I have to show you what real mumbo sauce tastes like anyway! No more of that imitation sauce you had me try a few weeks ago. I just can't believe you've lived here so long and have never had the real deal!"

"Well, I guess that ends today!" I say with excitement.

He grabs my waist and pulls me closer as I lean into him with his arms wrapped around me. Rubbing his arm, I glance up at him catching his eye. We stare into each other's eyes for several moments as Tamia's "Here Love I'm Yours" plays softly in the background, with every word she sings completely in tune with my heart in this moment. I felt vulnerable again, like there was still a chance at love for us because we both wanted it so bad.

"I don't know what's going to happen, but if you can be transparent with me from here on out, I'll always be in your corner," I tell him, breaking the silence.

Wiping the hair from my face, he responds, "I appreciate that. I want you and I'm going to make this work. I'm all in, no more lies."

Jay reaches over and grabs the back of my neck and pulls me closer until our lips meet again and again. We must've looked like two teenagers with raging hormones to the driver who was trying not to stare. A short while later we arrive at the restaurant. He decides to run in and get the food as I sit back in my seat to relax. As soon as his driver exits to smoke a cigarette, I feel a sudden vibration and the music stops playing simultaneously. I look down at the center console and realize that Jay left his phone connected to the auxiliary outlet and now the name of his ex, whom he claimed he'd blocked and hasn't talked to in months, was now displayed on his phone screen. Pissed, anxious, confused...every feeling imaginable began to race through my body as my heart began to beat quickly.

I look out of the window to my right to see Jay waiting at the counter for the food, then to my left to see the driver enjoying his cigarette. Finally, after a few moments, I give in. As soon as I press the answer button highlighted in green, it stops. I missed it. I missed her call and maybe the only opportunity to hear the truth because if she's still calling, Jay's word may not be as genuine as it sounds.

After nearly ten minutes, Jay comes back to the car with two bags of food.

"I got everything! But first, it's mumbo time!" he says, climbing back into car after setting the bags on the seat between us.

"You don't want to wait until we get back to your house?" I ask.

"Babe, it can't wait! You need to try some now, while it's hot!" he demands with a smile.

We both dig into the white plastic bag opening the styrofoam plates filled with fried chicken and the infamous mumbo dipping sauce. I pull the chicken from the bone, dipping it in the sauce trying my best to keep it together. I knew this wasn't the time to ask why his ex-fiancée from a year ago, was still calling.

"Oh my God...this is so good!" I say, surprised. Usually when people constantly tell you that you must try something, it rarely lives up to the hype. "Okay, you win! I'm a fan! No more imitation mumbo sauce from now on."

"Good! That's what I like to hear," Jay says. "So what do you want to do when we get back to my house?"

"I just want to relax, maybe watch a movie."

"Okay, but I'm not letting you pick this one out. Leave it to you we'll be watching Beaches and Love Actually for the millionth time and you'll be over there crying like you've never seen it before!" he chuckles.

"That's not funny! Those are two incredible movies. You just can't appreciate a good chick flick!" I passionately defend my love of sappy movies.

Thirty minutes later we pull into the driveway of his large estate after having devoured all of the chicken and mumbo sauce — all that was left were the bones. Still feeling a little uneasy, I keep up the facade that everything is okay as we make our way up the stairs and into his oversized bedroom. His room was massive and also had a lounging room adjacent to the bedroom which was separated by a double-sided fire place. I walk into the lounge area and plop down on the white sectional, scrolling through the movie channels hoping to find something that will catch my eye. Several minutes go by before I notice that Jay has disappeared. I stand up and head into his bedroom when I see candles lit in the distance, radiating from the attached bathroom. I walk down the walkway in his room leading into the bathroom, passing by multiple closets before I finally reach the end. Jay is sitting on the edge of his bubble bath filled Jacuzzi tub with his shirt off with candles lit, glowing all around him.

"Come here," he says, reaching for me.

As soon as I am close enough, he starts to undress me slowly until there was nothing left.

He drops his sweat pants to the floor then steps into the tub holding my hand, guiding me in after him. I lay there with him, cheek to cheek as his hands rub all over me, from my thighs to my breast. Though this moment was romantic and everything I could've hoped for, I wasn't mentally present. I allowed myself to check out emotionally as a way of protecting my heart. The only thing on my mind was that phone call. But still, it wasn't the right time, so we sat in the tub hugging and kissing on each other until our hands and feet grew soggy.

CHAPTER 20

The next morning, I roll over to find that Jay has already left for his early morning workout. I slide out of bed and walk towards the bathroom as the house phone begins to ring suddenly. I shuffle to the nearest phone to check the caller ID, thinking it was Jay calling. The name came onto the screen as unknown, but I noticed the California area code. Brushing it off, I went downstairs to make breakfast and check in with Taylor.

"Well hello, Ms. Davenport! So nice of you to return your best friend's call. This is starting to become a trend with you lately!"

"Oh, hush! It's only been a day."

"You're right; I just like to tease you. So what are you doing?" she asks.

"I'm over at Jay's making breakfast."

"Okay, so we're back on Jay now? Really, Dee?"

"Here we go," rolling my eyes, I immediately regret telling her where I was.

"One of these days you're going to listen to this good advice that people pay me for!" Taylor adds.

"I know, but the difference is, I didn't ask!"

"Okay! I just thought you were kicking him to the curb. What reeled you back in this time?" she questions further.

"He came over and we tried to talk things through. We just can't seem to shake each other. He promised that going forward, he would be totally honest."

"And you believed him?" Taylor asks, cutting me off.

"Obviously! I'm over his house cooking him breakfast in his tee shirt right now."

"Mmm, maybe you should've given him a chance to prove it before you took him at his word and hopped back into his bed. Especially since it looks like his ex just got to town. You know...the one whose name is tattooed on your man's body. But let me stop offering up advice you didn't ask for again!" she sarcastically responds.

"What are you talking about, Taylor?"

"I'm talking about her Twitter page. His ex from Cali that he was engaged to...remember her? Yeah, well she's in town and from her subliminal messages, either she's already seen Jay or she plans to."

"That's crazy," thinking to myself out loud, "she called his phone last night and I thought that was strange. Especially since Jay said he hasn't talked to her in a while and that he changed his number and supposedly blocked hers on his new line too just in case."

"Hmmm, I wonder how she got the new number. Could it be that, I don't know, he gave it to her because he's still very much in contact with her? Open your eyes, Dee! Don't give him the chance to hurt you again. The first time wasn't painful enough?"

"I'll call you back," I angrily hang up the phone slamming it against the granite topped kitchen island.

Standing there in the heart of his home, I try to collect my thoughts and work through my anger to get to a point of clarity. Aggravated, I stomp my way upstairs to the bedroom and shuffle through my oversized tote. I just need to escape. I decide the best thing to do is pack my things and leave. His morning workouts are usually a few hours long, so I figured that I have at least forty-five minutes before he gets back.

Before heading into the shower, I open the door to use the toilet. Clearly, Jay is a liar...still. Someone obviously wanted their presence to be known as they perfectly folded the toilet tissue ends over in a half diamond shape and left two strands of their long, dark hair strategically lying across the floor. This could've easily gone unnoticed as his bathroom was separated into his and hers sides, so the toilet areas were separately enclosed on opposite ends of the bathroom. Tears start to fall uncontrollably as Taylor's words echo in my mind. How could I be so naive and gullible? I feel like an idiot, yet again. I forgo a shower and make my way home as quickly as possible before I lose my temper and do something I might regret in a large house full of expensive breakables.

CHAPTER 21

After several days of ignoring Jay's persistent calls, they finally stopped. As silly as it sounds, a part of me wanted to call him back, especially once his calls mysteriously ended. This trip to see Josey couldn't have come at a better time. I could use a little L.A. weather to distract me from my current man woes.

Late as usual, Josey finally pulls up to the airport terminal where I've been sitting for the past thirty-five minutes, baking in the sun. I was border line annoyed, but I don't know what I expected. Being on time has never been her strong point, so I would usually have to tell her to be places at least thirty minutes earlier than she needed to be there, just so she'd get there on time. And sadly, even that didn't work half of the time.

"Hey, girl!" Josey yells out as she hops out of her all white Bentley.

"Hey, Josey! Thanks for being on time!" I say in a playful tone.

"I'm so sorry! It wasn't me this time! This L.A. traffic is the worst!"

"Yeah, yeah! Pop the trunk and take the top off of this convertible! Winter's depriving me of sunlight on the east coast, so I need to sink in every last ray of sun while I'm here."

We race down the 405 with the top down, embracing the breeze as it flows through our hair. I inhale deeply with a smile as the wind tickles my skin. The feeling is so refreshing. It's just what I need; the warm, relaxed climate that I can always count on California to provide. Before I know it, we're in the hills pulling up to Josey's swanky gated home. It was beautiful, like something you would see in the movies or showcased in Home & Garden magazine. It was so open with floor to ceiling windows lining the exterior, placed strategically at the highest point of the lot for the best view. Getting out of the car and walking up her steep driveway, I could only imagine how much greater the view must be from the inside looking out.

"Oh my God, Josey! I had no idea you were living this good!" Looking around, I was in awe of the gorgeous modern, yet rustic design of the house. "I'm slightly offended that you didn't invite me earlier! I would much rather prefer to drown my sorrows here than in the middle of snowy D.C.!"

"It is nice, isn't it?" she says emotionless, looking around slowly with a look of regret. "Too bad it all has to be packed up."

"What? I thought you guys just got this place earlier this year!"

"Yeah, we did," she responds nonchalantly. "Hey, but don't you feel like having one of our good ol' packing parties like we used to have back in the day when you moved every five minutes?"

"Ummm, not really!" I respond, with a perplexed look painted on my face.

"Ahhh, come on Dee! I've got the wine! Lots of it to go with the boxes and packing tape! How can you say no to anything with wine involved, huh?"

"You're the big baller around here, aren't you supposed to hire someone to do this for you?" I asked sarcastically, but clearly Josey wasn't amused. "What's going on anyway? You haven't mentioned anything about you guys moving."

"That's because 'we' are not moving," she pauses. Clearing her throat before slowly continuing, "What if I told you that when I drop you off at the airport that we'll actually be going home together on the same flight."

"What? I'm so lost right now, Josey. What are you saying?"

I follow her out to the back patio overlooking a pool so large that it would almost be suitable for Olympic swimmers to train.

"I'm leaving Garrett. I found a place right outside of D.C. that I love and I'm going to have this shit shipped there...right after you help me pack it all up," she says with a slight simper, patting me on my back. "I'm having my things shipped in three days before he gets home from a stretch of away games."

"Ummm...is this legal? You should really consider running this by Taylor because this sounds a little crazy and I'm not looking to be an accessory to any crimes!" I respond. "But seriously, is this how you want to leave things? This is a bit cold blooded — even for you!"

"Do I look like I care? I'm doing it!" She snaps then turns her back to me. Following her into the living room she tries to calm herself, still mumbling about Garrett under her breath. "I'm sure he'll have a new one in here decorating by this time next week anyway."

"Josey, stop. Sit down," I demand.

She sits next to me, stoic and emotionless as if she had truly given all that she had to this relationship and was physically unable to sacrifice another emotion or tear. I watch her as her eyes scan the room, seemingly in deep thought, realizing all that she would be leaving behind.

"All of this. This isn't me. I changed who I was for him all because I was scared that no one else would think I was good enough. For someone like him to not only notice me, but to marry me...I thought that I hit the jackpot and that everything would be perfect. I had no idea how much of myself I would have to sacrifice for someone who has no respect for me and would rather spend his nights in a club full of strangers than to come home. The part that's even crazier..." she hesitates for a moment, grasping her mouth as tears start to fall. I console her, rubbing her back as she tries to continue. "After trying for the past two years unsuccessfully, I just found out that I'm three weeks pregnant; I can't even be happy! I feel so guilty and low that the thought of terminating my pregnancy has crossed my mind more than once. I'm so scared, Dee. I've created such a mess for myself. I should've left a long time ago," shaking her head at her own bad decisions, "It should've never come to this."

For once, I was at a loss for words. In complete shock, I sat there holding on firmly to Josey as she grew more distant and her eyes began to swell with tears again and again until she was physically incapable of sacrificing another tear.

A few hours later, after Josey was able to compose herself, the packing began. Box after box, wine bottle after wine bottle consistently until the third and final bottle was empty. By this time it was after midnight. I suggested we finish my last glass of wine and her last glass of apple cider by the pool and then get some rest so we could get an early start in the morning. We walk to the edge of the pool and dip our feet in the warm water that flowed just below our knees. I watch Josey silently for a few minutes, trying to read her current state of mind before I spoke. Her eyes roamed across the night sky before resting on the moon illuminated in the distance.

"Man, where does the time go?" she says with a subtle disposition. "It seems like just yesterday we were flying all over the world, baiting these poor boys for fun! Well, I was anyway. I still need to teach you the game apparently," she jokes.

"Tell me about it! We were so young. I can't believe it's been ten years." The reality of my words starts to set in as I take another sip of wine. "You and Gia were the worst though!"

We both laugh inseparably thinking back to all the good times we shared before the mood takes a shift.

"What happened to us, Dulsey?"

"I wish I had the answers. I bet if our younger selves could see us now, they wouldn't even recognize the women we've become," I sighed.

"Isn't that the scary truth? I just hope I can find myself. I don't ever want to lose myself in a man again the way I have with Garrett. That's the complete opposite of how I lived my life back then and I want to get back to her. She was pretty damn amazing!"

"I mean, she was okay!" I joke, to lighten the mood.

"Oh hush, you know you loved her!"

"I did! And I still do," pulling her in close and holding onto her tightly.

"Thanks for always having my back. I really don't know what I would do without you."

"You'll always have me, so you'll never have to worry about that. Always."

"But enough about me and my astronomical drama! How are things with you and Jay?"

"I think I need another bottle of wine if we start talking about that man, so why don't we just call it a night."

Taken aback by my response and unsure of how to react, Josey follows me back into the house. We don't speak another word as we retreat to our bedrooms separately. I return to the guest room to find a missed call from Jay. I close the bedroom door and wrestle with the thought of calling him back for a few moments before it dawns on me that his ex is still in town and it's his off day. I decide to face time him, but he declines it each time which left me feeling nervous. He always answers my face time requests, especially at this hour. There's no reason he shouldn't be free to answer my call — unless he's preoccupied with someone else.

I struggle to fall asleep even though I was beyond exhausted from packing most of the day. I keep imagining all the things that Jay is up to and if there's someone keeping him company while I'm away. This uneasy feeling was starting to really nag me, so I sent Taylor a text message asking her for her login information so I can hopefully put my mind at ease. Not even five minutes later Taylor calls me instead of just texting me back. This can't be good.

"Hey Taylor, I take it you got my text!"

"Girl, did I! Are you sitting down?"

"Oh no, just lay it on me," dreading the words that have yet to come out of her mouth.

"I'm sending over some screenshots and well, you just tell me whose bathroom this is before I jump to any conclusions for you."

As soon as I pull the phone away from my ear, I look down at it and open up the image Taylor sent. Sure enough the picture was taken in Jay's large tub with bubbles and rose peddles strategically placed, spelling out 'I love u' with a heart in place of the word love. My heart sank into my stomach. I took a moment before placing the phone back to my ear.

"Dee, you okay?" Taylor asks.

"Yeah, I don't know why I'm so surprised. I felt it all along. I just knew something wasn't right."

"I assume this was posted on her page."

"Yep."

"Unbelievable."

"I know it's not what you wanted to see, but at least you know for sure. You don't have to worry yourself to death making assumptions!" Taylor adds.

"Thanks, Taylor. I think I'm just going to try to sleep this off. I'm so tired of stressing over this pitiful excuse of a man."

"Okay, Dee. If you need me, just call. Goodnight."

"Night," hanging up the phone with a heavy heart.

The next morning I wake up to not a single missed call or text from Jay. He must still be busy professing his love for his ex. As I exit the guest room, I find Josey up early getting a head start on packing up the master bedroom. Not wanting to add to her stress, I keep my drama to myself and start packing boxes right next to her.

We commence to packing up the remainder of the house, finishing up late that night. To celebrate the closing of one chapter, we head over to the trendy West Hollywood area for a late dinner. We found a nice little tapas restaurant and were seated in the dimly lit bar area with the perfect view of all of the beautiful people congregating nearby.

Just as my first round of martinis hit the table, Josey's interrogation begins out of nowhere as she sips happily on her water.

"So, what has Jay done now?" she asks.

I attempt to shrug off her question, not sure if I was ready to talk about my feelings because they were still basically based on assumptions at this point.

"Really, Dee! No response? Well, I don't like how you ended our conversation last night and how you've been skirting the topic all day. Just talk to me!"

"I really don't know what to say," I admit, with a sigh of frustration. "It's just so odd. It's like we get to a place where things feel great and then his past pops up in some form or another and ruins all the progress we've made every single time!"

"What happened after you and Taylor found out all that stuff about his ex-girlfriend?"

"Well, of course he made it seem like she was just talking and dwelling on the past, but he missed the entire reason that I was mad to begin with. He never told me half of the things that I had to find out over the internet."

"Oh, he got it. He just tip toed around it for minimal damage to your situation. You have to realize you're dealing with a different breed! These athletes start to feel so entitled. And you know with that sense of entitlement comes a plethora of women with no morals or values willing to do whatever, whenever for a bag, shoes, or just a chance to be in their presence. It's pitiful, but they get so used to not having to say no, but find a way to cover it up so it looks like nothing ever happened so you're left feeling like the crazy one."

"Yeah, I'm starting to notice that with Jay. I just never knew one person could have so many sides to them, but I guess anything is possible nowadays."

"I'm proof. Get out while you can!"

We shared a toast and then many more followed as we spilt several appetizers, nostalgic of the old times we shared. The next afternoon the movers were at her house promptly at noon to pick up all of her belongings. As they took each box, I could see it chip away at her. Even though she knew deep down she had to go, there was still something so familiar that she'd become so accustomed to that she was scared to leave behind.

As they loaded the last box, our car service arrives to take us both to the airport. Josey leaves the keys to her Bentley along with the house and gate keys on the kitchen counter with a brief note that read, "I just couldn't live a lie anymore. xoxo Josey".

Unbeknownst to Garrett, he would return to a hollow home...just like the inside of Josey's heart.

CHAPTER 22

By this time, winter had come and gone and spring is transitioning into summer. Josey's belly is growing rapidly and our bond was tighter than ever. Having her nearby strengthened our bond, making it more solid than it had ever been. Taylor was still slick at the mouth offering up advice that no one asked for and Gia finally freed herself from her unhealthy relationship with Anthony. I cut Jay off completely once I returned home from L.A. I opted to break up over the phone this time to prevent any bad decisions that could've come from a weak moment of actually being in his presence. My dad and I have taken turns visiting one another and he's even accompanied me to brunch a couple times with the girls. Life has really taken a turn for the best for everyone.

It was my dad's last night in town, so all the girls came over to my place to help me prepare dinner for him. My girls know I've always been a little challenged when it comes to having culinary skills, so with preparing a dinner of this magnitude their help was much needed and appreciated. We all sat around the kitchen island waiting for the last few side dishes to bake in the oven as we all indulged in our second glass of wine and grape juice for Josey.

"You know, Dee, I'm glad your dad has become such a big part of your life again. I think we've all kind of adopted him as our own father too!" Josey giggles.

"Yes, he definitely always offers up a great, solid male perspective so we don't have to rely on ol' big mouth over here all the time!" Gia laughs, slyly pointing at Taylor.

"Oh, honey please! I know what I'm talking about! Why do you think I'm the only one that's never crying over a man," Taylor defends herself.

"Because you're scared to let a man in my darling!" my father interrupts as he enters the kitchen mid-conversation with two more bottles of wine in tow. "But there's nothing wrong with waiting to let your guard down for the right man, so don't let the girls tell you otherwise!"

"Oh, I won't Robert!" she responds, playfully sticking her tongue out at us.

"It smells so good in here, you ladies have outdone yourselves! This feels like Thanksgiving!" my dad says with the biggest grin as his eyes scan the countertops filled with food.

"Have a seat, I'll pour you a glass while we wait for dinner to finish," I say.

As I run over to the oven to check on the casserole, Josey blurts out of nowhere, "I heard from Garrett today."

"And what did he say?" Gia inquires as we all stare fixedly waiting for her response.

"Well," she pauses, breathing slowly and trying to hold back tears, "he said that when the baby comes, I shouldn't get too attached because he and his new girlfriend are going to fight me tooth and nail for full custody."

"What?"

"That bastard!" Gia says consoling Josey.

"I don't know what I'm going to do! One minute he doesn't want anything to do with us, the next he wants to take everything I have!" she continues.

"Sweetheart, it sounds like that is his cowardly way of trying to hurt you the way you hurt him when you left and took everything. He wants to do whatever is in his power to make you hurt. I'm sure he feels like with his money he can do whatever he wants, but you've got a good one fighting for you," my father says, grabbing Taylor's shoulder as he refers to her.

"He's exactly right, Josey. I don't want you to waste another tear or thought on that man. That's my job!" Taylor reminds her. "Don't worry! We're going to hit him where it counts. And that's in the courtroom, honey, so don't mind his idle threats!"

"You're right, I'm sorry for bringing it up. It's just been on my mind all day since he called."

"It's okay, we totally understand!" Gia says.

"Did he even ask how the baby was doing or did he call just throw jabs?" I ask.

"He never asks about the baby. He even had the nerve to make a comment like there's a possibility that it's not his because I never got pregnant in the two years that we were actually trying before."

"I'm so sorry you have to go through this, sweetheart. We men can be so selfish and caught up in our own feelings sometimes that we forget how fragile and valuable you all are. Just try not to let this taint your heart. After all you are going to be raising a young man very soon!" Robert says.

Josey rubs her belly and immediately begins to smile, "You're right, I won't let him win."

The timer on the oven goes off, so we gather the remaining dishes and bring them to the dinner table. We all sit down, say grace, and break bread sharing stories all night long. Each time I look around, I smile a little bigger inside. Just to have all of the people I love in the same room together filled me with joy and gave me hope that other aspects of my life are sure to fall into place too.

After two and a half hours of dinner, conversation, and several bottles of wine, we all finally decide to call it a night. As I walk my father to his rental car, he chimes in on how happy I appear.

"It's so good to see you smiling this much! It really makes me happy and eases my worry."

"Awww, Dad! You don't have to worry about me. I'm going to be just fine!"

"I know, baby girl. Whoever gets you is getting the ultimate prize! You are amazing and so deserving of the best."

"Thanks Dad, I love you."

"Love you, too! I'll give you a call when I get back home. And your sisters are excited to come back with me before school starts!"

"Tell them I send my love! I can't wait to take them on a tour of the city. It's going to be so much fun."

"Will do. I'm sure they're just as excited as you are!"

"Have a safe flight!"

Closing his door and stepping away from the driveway, I wave at my father as he pulls off. Closing the front door behind me, I can hear the girls laughing and conversing as I make my way back into the kitchen.

"Thanks so much for your help guys, I really appreciate it!"

"Oh no problem. Robert is great, so of course we would help out and send him off in style with a full belly!" Gia says.

"I almost forgot!" Taylor interrupts, "There's a gala I have to go to this weekend for one of my firm's clients. He's actually kind of cute, so I wouldn't mind making an appearance. Does anyone want to come with me?"

"If I didn't feel like I was 500 pounds with a 'wide load' sign stamped on my behind, I would. But with this pregnancy, all I ever want to do is sleep on the weekends! Sorry!" Josey says.

"I understand. What about you two?" Taylor asks staring at Gia and me.

"I actually have a date this weekend, so count me out for this one!" Gia responds.

"Wait, why haven't we heard about this guy?" I ask.

"It's our first date, so there's nothing to tell yet!" she shrugs.

"Okay, so it looks like it's just me and you, Dee! What do you say?"

"Sure, I don't have any plans and it gives me a reason to shop for a new dress. I'm in!"

"Great! I'll pick you up at six on Saturday then!"

———

It was five-thirty and I was hopping around my bedroom in full black tie attire after stubbing my toe on the bed post. I finally give into the pain, falling over onto the mocha colored chaise parallel to my bed. Just as the pain begins to subside, the phone rings.

I brace myself for a moment before limping over to answer the call.

"Hey Taylor, I'm almost ready!"

"Good, I was calling to make sure you weren't running late! I got us a driver for the night and we should be pulling up in about twenty minutes."

"Okay, I'll be ready."

I pull my other Jimmy Choo pump from underneath the bed and slide my foot into it. Taylor pulls up in a black sedan just as I finish stuffing my tiny clutch full of lipstick, gum, and credit cards. I grab my keys and dart out of the door.

"Oh my goodness! Why did I not realize that it was starting to drizzle? I didn't prepare for this!" I blurt out as soon as I step into the car.

"Sweetie, it's okay. The driver has an umbrella and I'll make sure he makes it his duty to keep the rain away from those curls!"

"See, that's why I love you!" I lean in and give her a hug and greet her properly. "So you never told me why you were so pressed to come out to this gala. Usually you're the one coming up with any excuse to wiggle your way out of these types of events."

"You know that if I make it a point to go to one of these functions, there has to be a damn good reason!" she laughs. "After so many years of the same faces and fake facades, I thought I had seen it all and I was pretty much over it. I didn't feel like it was benefiting me in any way and I was just going through the motions. But then two weeks ago this handsome tall drink of water walks into our office and personally invites us all to his event."

"Wait! I'm just excited to hear that you're excited about a man! I was starting to wonder about you," I say, looking at her out of the corner of my eye raising one eyebrow.

"Honey, please! Only a real man could handle all of this!"

"You're right about that one, Taylor! I hope he's ready."

Flipping open her compact, she begins running her fingers through her hair before responding, "I hope he is too! It's been too long."

We pull up to the valet in front of the museum where the gala is being held and we are carefully guided into the building, as the driver hovers over us with a large black umbrella. Everything about this place is amazing, from the elegant decor to the waiters walking around with an assortment of delectable appetizers and champagne. Taylor tugs on my hand as a tall, handsome man approaches, signaling that this was the man I had just gotten an ear full about.

"Doug! How are you?" Taylor yells out as she approaches him with open arms.

"Doug? Talk about a name not matching a face," I mumble to myself before she pulls me closer and introduces us. I then step back and allow them to chat amongst themselves as it was clear that the interest and admiration was mutual between the two. Shortly after, Doug is called to the stage to give a speech. Taylor and I take that as our cue to find our seats.

We make our way through the crowd and find our seats quickly, which have the perfect view of the stage, just off center as Doug steps up to the podium to speak. Taylor is so enamored with Doug, hanging on his every word as he delivers his brief speech and thanks everyone for attending. Just watching her allowing herself to be open with a man is so refreshing. After the death of her fiancé, their son became her entire world and she never felt that anyone could live up to the standards of her first and only true love.

I look over at her and tease, "Doug, huh?"

Unable to contain her laughter, she responds, "I figured if I led with his name, you would be envisioning some stiff, nerdy guy with glasses!"

"Yeah, I would've! It's just such an injustice...poor guy! His parents should be glad that he turned out to be so good looking!"

"Fuck!" Taylor sighs with an annoyed look on her face.

"Taylor, I'm sorry! I was just kidding!"

"Dee, it's not that."

"Well, what is it?"

Confused, I turn and look over my shoulder to figure out what's causing Taylor to react this way. Just as I shift far enough in my seat, I see a friend of ours named Jaime who is a publicist in the area making her way over to our table...with Jay.

"Hello ladies! I haven't seen you girls in so long!" Jamie says, genuinely excited to see us.

With a long, drawn out, "Hey!" we both respond in unison trying to seem unbothered by Jay's presence.

"Oh, girls, I want you to meet Jay Waters! He's my new client, so I'm taking him out to events and showing him the ropes."

Unable to put on a fake smile any longer, I respond, "Oh, we've met. And he made quite an impression. If you'll excuse me," I brush past Jay heading towards the restroom. I felt myself getting emotionally worked up just at the sight of him and I didn't want to give him the pleasure of witnessing my breakdown firsthand.

I thought I had closed that chapter, but somehow he keeps finding a way to have a reoccurring role in my book of life.

CHAPTER 23

I pause before exiting the restroom to take a deep breath. Clearly I wouldn't be able to completely avoid Jay, but I plan to try. I was so torn because I was ready to leave, but I didn't want to ruin this night for Taylor and Doug. I pull myself together and put on my big girl panties, so to speak, and decide to stick it out. As soon as the door swings open, I see Jay standing there waiting patiently. He notices me, so I try to speed past him to make it back to my table without making eye contact, let alone have a conversation. Just as I walk past him, he gently grabs my hand to get my attention.

"Dulsey, please! I just need a moment of your time and then I'll leave you alone!" he pleads.

I turn around and face him, only to realize that our time away has been good to him. He was well put together and perfectly groomed in his black tuxedo and bow tie. He finally even cut off that small beard of his that I hated so much.

"Jay, we really don't have anything to talk about. Things happened the way they were supposed to — the end. Have a good night and I hope not see you for the rest of it," I say boldly, then turn to walk back to my table. Unaware of where I gathered the strength to walk away, I couldn't help but smile to myself at this small victory.

I sat back down at the table next to a concerned Taylor who was waiting to hear all of the details.

"I figured you could hold your own...just in case you wanted that alone time with him," Taylor explains.

"It's okay, I'm a big girl. I handled it. Nothing to tell," shrugging my shoulders.

Respecting the vibe that I was giving off that I didn't want to talk about it, she quickly changes the subject.

"So while you were away, Doug stopped by the table and asked me out for drinks afterwards. Would you mind if I went with him when the gala ends? I can have the driver take you straight home."

"Of course! I don't mind at all, Taylor. Doug seems like a great guy, so go get your happily ever after. You deserve it," I say with a faint smile, still bothered by my run in with Jay.

"Thank you, Dee! I love you girl!"

Taylor embraces me with the biggest grin. We devour our delicious meals; tender lamb with potatoes and asparagus, trying not to lick the plate as amazing as it tastes. We then mingle with a few friends we haven't seen in a while over the course of the next hour before we start to wrap up the evening. I can sense Taylor's excitement as we chit chat in the lobby while we wait for Doug to break free from his obligations. He walks over a few minutes later and takes Taylor to his sleek, black Porsche parked out front. I walk out of the lobby and into the front garden area as I wait for the driver to pull around when I see a familiar black SUV parked directly in front of me. The black rear tinted window rolls down slowly to reveal Jay's eyes.

"Hey, Dulsey."

"Really? Again?"

"I know earlier wasn't the right time, but can we talk now?"

"Actually, my car will be pulling up any moment so I'm not sure now will work either."

"Please, are you sure you can't spare a few minutes? That's all I ask."

I look around trying to think of any excuse as it starts to rain. He gets out of the SUV and approaches me once again taking off his jacket and putting it over my head to shield me from the rain. "Come on, get in. I don't want you to get wet. You can wait in my car," he says, excusing the driver as soon as the door closes behind me. Wasting not one single moment, he starts in, "Look I know I didn't handle things the right way the last time I saw you..."

"No, it's...it's fine. It really is," I interrupt him not wanting to dredge up the past.

"You were everything to me. You were so good to me even when I didn't deserve it and I just kept messing things up time after time," he continues on anyway.

"It's really okay. We don't have to go there. It happened and it's over, let's just leave things there and move on."

"Dulsey, let me finish! Please!" He pauses for a moment to collect his thoughts before starting again, "Since that night I've been thinking a lot about us and how good we were together and I..."

"Look, seriously, you really don't have to do this! It didn't work out, you weren't ready, so let's just let it go." I notice my driver finally pulling up so I prepare to exit. I glance over to see the look of confusion on Jay's face, as if he was at a loss for words. I continue, "We're good. Everything's okay, so let's just leave it there. My car is here, so I'm gonna go now." I look down to avoid eye contact, then quickly slide out of the back of the SUV. Before I can close the door behind me, he places his hand against the door preventing it from closing.

"Can we at last meet for dinner tomorrow?" he persists.

"No."

"Drinks? Anything?"

I stop, consumed with frustration and beginning to get upset as the rain lightly pours down on me. "So 'no' just doesn't work anymore, huh? Okay, so let me make this clear for you! We can't go to dinner or have drinks! I want nothing to do with you...that's it!"

"I apologize! I only want to see you happy, that's all."

"You want to see me happy? Then disappear from my life again, except this time stay gone. Okay? Just take care and let me be."

"Wait, Dulsey! Wait!" he yells out, chasing after me just as I reach my car service. "So this is it?"

I prepare to get into the back of the black sedan before turning around to address Jay one last time. "Jay, do you hear me begging to be back in your life or questioning you about your child's mother and that whole mess? Huh? No, never and do you know why? Because I don't care! There is no 'us' anymore, you made sure of that a long time ago so don't act like you care so much about me all of a sudden. You had your chance, so yeah, have a nice life...without me."

I hop into the backseat and the driver closes the door behind me, leaving Jay standing on the curb dumbfounded. I fell over into a fettle position on the black leather seats, grasping my knees into my chest as tears start to flow uncontrollably down my face and onto my expensive gown. All I could do is wonder what it all means. Was life going too well? Was I a little too happy?

Fighting the urge to tell the driver to turn around so I could see Jay one last time, I reach for my cell phone stuffed securely in my clutch instead.

I needed a voice of reason. I dialed my father.

Barely able to hold back tears, as soon as he answers, "I need to hear it! I need to hear that I'm strong and I'm making the right decision. Please!"

"Baby girl, what's wrong? Why are you crying and what decision are you talking about?"

"I can't talk about it right now; I just need your reassurance. I just need to be reminded not to go back to that place...that place of unhappiness."

"Oh, sweetheart. You are a prize, you are the light at the end of a dark tunnel, you are strong, and I trust that any decision you make is the best one for you. Whatever it is that you are wrestling with, be strong and let it go. If it's not bringing a smile to your beautiful face, peace to your heart, or positivity into your life then you've made the right decision."

"Thank you," I respond trying to calm myself, drying my tears. "I really needed to hear that."

"Get some rest and call me tomorrow when you've had a chance to work through whatever it is that's got you down. Okay?"

"Okay. Goodnight."

I've come too far to end up back in his circle of chaos. As the driver parks in front of my house, I take a moment to get myself together long enough to make it through the front door. I made it to the sofa and pull the chevron patterned throw over my legs, closing my eyes as tightly as possible hoping I would just fall asleep and forget this day ever happened.

——

The next morning Taylor calls bright and early, eager to dish on how her evening went with Doug.

"Wake up, woman! I have got some good news for you...about me, of course!" she says anxiously.

"Uh huh! I imagine all of this energy at eight in the morning has everything to do with your new beau."

"You would be correct! Dee, this is so exciting! After Michael passed, I never looked at another man romantically in the way that I did with Doug last night. I wasn't sure it would happen for me, but I think this might be my second chance at love."

"Wow, wow! Now before we start planning the wedding, can I at least get all the details from last night first?" I laugh to myself at Taylor's out of character behavior. She's normally the cynical one, not the goo goo gaga, mushy type.

"Okay, well after the charity event, he took me to the rooftop of this restaurant downtown where he arranged for it to stay open after their closing hours just for us! When we stepped off of the elevator, he took me through a series of glass doors that led to this beautiful balcony that stretched around the entire side of the building. And in the corner, with views of the monuments, there was a table set up for two with chocolate covered strawberries and champagne."

"Wait, wait, wait..." I interrupt, "Does he have a brother...cousin...friend?"

"Hush, Dee!"

"Sorry, just curious! Continue!"

"We sat there for the next couple hours laughing, talking about our personal lives and our careers and what we wanted out of life. It just felt good to be on the same page with someone for once. Just to be able to have an in depth conversation about life and be so into it that you lose all track of time was so invigorating. Oh, and I forgot to mention, I'm sure you'll think it was corny, but about an hour in, he had a violinist come and serenade us as we danced."

"Shut up! I don't believe you!"

"Girl, if it didn't happen to me I wouldn't believe me either! The amount of time and effort that he put into making our first evening together so special, actually made me want to believe in love again after being numb to it for so long...but I..." she stops herself, hesitating to finish her sentence. "It's just so annoying...but I keep waiting for the other shoe to drop! I don't want to feel like this is too good to be true, but it's definitely in the back of my mind."

"Taylor, you've been through a lot and you've sort of used your hurt as armor when it comes to men. I'm just glad you found a wonderful man who's willing to fight through that tough exterior to get to your heart and make you feel again. I love you and I have no doubts that he will too if you allow him to."

"Thanks, Dee. I really needed to hear that. I think I'm going to get out of my own way this time and just see where things go."

"I think that's a great idea."

I let Taylor gush on for another hour about her amazing night with Doug and kept my little incident with Jay to myself. It was her moment, a moment of happiness she hadn't felt in so long and I didn't want to bring any rain to her parade.

I spent the rest of the morning cleaning up around the house before taking the afternoon off to rest my mind and my body. The weather was so nice and breezy that I let up all the windows in the house to enjoy the fresh air as I get cozy on the couch, flipping through channels and enjoying a glass of fresh sangria.

Out of the blue, my doorbell rings just as I was about to find out who's being eliminated this week on my favorite guilty pleasure reality show. Slightly annoyed, I pause the show and roll over on the couch far enough to get a clear view of who is outside my front door. Lo and behold it's my honorary fifth "girlfriend", Leon...or Leona, depending on what day of the week it is. Leon is our very flamboyant, over the top, homosexual friend from work that we fell in love with the very first day we met him. His energy is always so high and his attitude is always positive. It's impossible to have a bad day or even a dull one in his presence, which is why we welcomed him into our circle with open arms years ago.

I hop up in my grey sweats and oversized tee shirt to greet Leon at the door with a hug and a kiss on each cheek.

"Leon, what are you doing here? Feels like it's been forever!"

"Darling, me and Drew got into it and I had to leave! I hope you don't mind me just dropping by like this, unexpected!"

"No, not at all! I was just catching up on some reality television, nothing special."

"Good! Now where can I get a glass of whatever that is that you're drinking?"

"Got you covered," I yell out over my shoulder as I run into the kitchen.

"Fill mine to brim though, honey!"

"The brim? That stressed, huh?"

"You have no idea," he says as I walk back into the living room with a full glass of sangria. "I may need to crash here tonight...unless I get picked up off of Craig's List first," he adds, jokingly. At least I think he was joking.

"You are too much! So what did Drew do to get you this riled up?"

"So I'm supposed to be gone on this trip for work for four days, and you know my schedule is posted on the fridge so Drew can keep up with it. We ended up having some weather issues and my flights got canceled, so I finished up a day early. I'm thinking, great! I can surprise Drew and be there when he gets home from work and have dinner cooked and the whole nine." He pauses to take a dramatic sigh followed by a gulp of his drink before he continues, "I get home and I'm already irritated because the place is a mess. I walk upstairs and into our bedroom to find Drew in bed with another man and I lost it!"

"Oh, no! He isn't dead, is he?" (Because with Leon, this is a question that needs to be asked)

"No, girl. But I can't say that wasn't the goal for those ten seconds that I was seeing red though! It turned into a big shoving match where Drew was trying to get me under control and keep me calm long enough for the guy to get his stuff and leave. As soon as he let me up, I packed a bag and left. I drove around for a little while to calm down and then I came here."

"I'm so sorry to hear that! You came to the right place though, because you know I live on 'can't catch a break with love' avenue, so I feel your pain."

Leon continues to gulp his sangria down as if he was drinking water before he stops and comes up for air, "Mmm, this drink is great but please tell me you have something stronger in that kitchen somewhere," he says wiping his mouth.

"Yeah, I'm sure there's some vodka in the back cabinet," standing up to go search for alcohol.

"Okay, no you stay put and I'll play bartender. Oh, and ice cream?"

"There should be some in the freezer," I shout out from my little nook on the couch.

"Perfect, because no pity party is complete without booze and ice cream!" he yells out from the kitchen.

Chapter 24

Two days pass and both mornings I managed to wake up with a headache and a hangover from all of the mixed drinks and ice cream Leon and I consumed. I walk downstairs to find Leon wide awake brewing coffee in the kitchen.

"Morning love!" he greets me with a smile.

"Good morning. Why are you so damn happy?" I ask, as I watch him prance around the kitchen. "We're alive and breathing, honey! That puts me in a good mood every morning!"

"Rub some of that happiness off on me, please!"

"How'd you sleep?"

"I think I over indulged last night, but I slept like a baby. Now this headache, I could do without! No more alcohol and ice cream tonight, I need a break!"

"Well, I actually wanted to talk to you about that. Looks like I'll be out of your hair in a few," Leon says walking around the kitchen table to sit down next to me. "Drew called this morning and we talked. Like really talked, which I feel like we haven't done in weeks. We've been having issues for a while now and we both agreed that we have some things that we really need to work through if we're going to stay together. By the end of the conversation we agreed to go to counseling and see if we can salvage this thing," he says in a tone that was hard for me to read. "I feel like we have so much of our lives intertwined that the only choice I have is to figure it out, you know?"

"That's a tough space to be in. Do you feel trapped in your relationship or do you genuinely want to be in it and feel like it's worth fighting for?"

"I wish I had a clear answer, but I think it's a little of both. I mean, I can always leave but we've made so many decisions together that would make it a little more difficult. Like we just bought a house together and we have joint accounts; everything you shouldn't do before getting a ring is exactly what we did, just being dumb and in love. But, I do still love him and I feel like there's a glimmer of hope in it for us. And I guess a glimmer is better than nothing."

"At least you guys were able to talk about it calmly and handle things like adults. I really hope everything works out. You're too amazing to be with anyone who doesn't treat you well and value you as a person."

"Thanks, sweetie! That applies to you as well, you know!"

I giggle, "Yeah? I'm not quite sure I'm as forgiving as you are at this point. But then again, Drew didn't pop up with a baby!"

"Honey, this is true! But if Jay isn't the one, don't close yourself off to the possibility of love with someone else. You never know when love will find you!"

We hug for a few moments and suddenly I felt lonely at the thought of going back to a pity party for one. Having company the last couple days has been a welcomed distraction from reality for the both of us, I'm sure.

Leon whips up a light breakfast for us both as we sit and talk more in depth about his relationship and where he hopes things will go. I admire him so much for not being afraid to jump back into love after being hurt so deeply. I'm not sure if I have developed that level of resiliency, especially with the way things went with Jay the other night. Listening to Leon made me want to be smarter about my decisions when it comes to love but I still seem to have that soft spot for Jay. Seeing him again was like reopening an old wound that never did heal quite right in the first place.

I pick up the plates and wash them as Leon repacks his overnight bag.

"Okay, lady. I think that's the last of my stuff. I'm going to go throw this in the car and then I'll be back for my smooch!"

I smile at how silly he was being and watch him walk out to the car. He slings his bag in the backseat then walks around the rear of the car to hop in the front seat and let the top down on his convertible Mustang. The breeze was starting to pick up to alleviate some of the heat, and it was the perfect day to be outdoors and take in the weather. Just as he gets out and starts to walk back towards me, I see him do a double take glancing over his right shoulder at the black SUV parked in front of my house.

He walks back in with a look of concern on his face before stating, "Ummm...I think you have a stalker."

"What? A stalker?"

"Yeah. You don't find it odd that this SUV has been parked there for the past hour? And there's clearly someone sitting in the driver's seat and a guy in the back."

"I didn't notice it. It's probably just a driver picking up one of my neighbors. I'm not really worried about it."

"Are you sure?" he asks.

"Yeah, I'm sure. I'll be fine."

"Okay, darling. Well, if you need me just give me a buzz. I'll call you when I get home, okay?"

"Okay, Leon. Drive safe!" I say, embracing him before he rushes off to his car. I step outside onto my front steps to see him off.

Just as he pulls out of the driveway, the driver gets out and walks around to the back passenger side door of the mysterious SUV. The door swings open and I see a well dressed gentleman in a grey pinstriped, tailored suit step onto the sidewalk. In an attempt not to stare too hard, I turn and start to walk back into the front door. I look back one final time to find that he's making his way towards me. I glance up and see that it's Jay clutching two dozen red, long stemmed roses. Out of sheer shock I stop dead in my tracks. He approaches me and extends the flowers towards me before greeting me in such a gentle tone, "Hi Dulsey. I know I'm the last person you want to see right now, but I refuse to let you go without a fight."

"So you thought a fancy suit and some flowers were going to make everything okay again?" I ask, genuinely wanting an honest response. I ease back, reaching for the door handle. He grabs my hand and I turn my head back to face him.

"Can you honestly look me in my face and say you don't love me or want to be with me?" he asks, "Because if you can, then I'll leave right now and you'll never have to worry about me again."

"Yeah, right. I've heard that line from you before and yet here you are again!" I say, throwing my hands up. "Why? Huh? Why come back into my life when you see that I'm happy and that I'm trying to move on? What is it?" I stare into his eyes waiting for a response, but his lips remain closed, tightly. "Say something! I need to understand. What is it? Is it that you see, damn, Dulsey might actually be happy, let me find a way to fuck this up for her? Is that it?" I continue to question to no avail. I turn away from him, tilting my head back hoping to prevent the tears that are bubbling up in my eyes, from falling.

"I came here because you're not happy," he finally mutters.

"And how would you know that?"

"Because I saw how happy you were when you were with me and I know I can make you that happy again. I messed up and I own that! I've grown so much in our time apart and I've cleared out all of the skeletons in my closet so that when the time came, we could truly start fresh. I just need the chance to make things right with us once and for all."

"Us? Jay, you don't listen. For the last time, there is no us!" I express, glaring at him. "You don't get to do this to me again! You don't get to pull my strings like I'm your little puppet! Not this time."

"It's different this time, Dulsey!"

"It's never different! You know that."

He looks down for a moment and reaches into the inside pocket of his suit jacket and pulls out a small, charcoal colored box. Looking me directly in the eyes, he says, "Does this show you that it will be different this time — that I'm different this time."

He opens the box and kneels down on one knee. Inside is the most flawless princess cut diamond ring I have ever laid my eyes on. He calls out my name in an attempt to get my attention, being that I was so blindsided by the ring. "Dulsey Alexandra Davenport, will you do me the ultimate honor of being my wife?" After a few moments go by, he asks again, "Dulsey, please! Will you marry me?" Jay stands up and grasps my hands waiting for a response. After the initial shock starts to wear off and the silence lingers, reality sets in.

"I don't think I can do this," I utter quietly before turning around and running into the house. Jay follows behind me searching for answers.

"I know we have some things to figure out, but it's just me and you now! Just us! We were always good when it was just us. Remember? Tell me you remember!" he pleads.

"I do...but I also remember all of the pain that followed. A baby is a hard pill to swallow and I'm not even sure if I'm ready for that type of responsibility!" I admit.

"No, that's over. It's done! You don't have to worry about that anymore!"

"What?"

"It's done! It's just us again, how it should've been. Come here, baby. Please!"

I walk over to him slowly and he pulls me in close as he whispers in my ear, "Dulsey, say you'll be my wife and stick with me from here on out through thick and thin. I love you and the only person that I plan to have my child, is you."

With my head planted in his chest and a million things going through my mind, I finally respond.

"Okay."

He pulls away and holds me by my shoulders hoping that he heard me correctly, as I smile and reassure him that I wanted to be his wife. I finally understood what Leon was feeling. The heart wants what the heart wants and sometimes even a small glimmer of hope is all you need...

CHAPTER 25

Several weeks have passed and Jay and I were finally getting to a happier, more comfortable place in our lives and in our relationship. The girls weren't too keen on me giving him another chance and accepting his marriage proposal after our rocky patch, but as time goes by they're slowly starting to come around and be supportive of my decision to move forward with this relationship. My parents, on the other hand, still need more convincing than anyone. My father, especially, isn't yet sold on the fact that Jay is a changed man and ready for marriage. So in an effort to smooth things over with the wedding fast approaching, I invited the girls and my father over for dinner so they can all meet face to face and really see firsthand that Jay isn't the bad guy and that he really has grown in our time apart.

With me finally moving most of my things into his large mansion, it was starting to feel like home. This was a huge milestone for me, and to commemorate this huge step, Jay came up with the idea to have everyone over to host a dinner in *our* home for the first time. It felt amazing to know that he was so attentive to how I was feeling and I was even more so impressed to see that he's putting forth an immense amount of effort to make things work smoothly. We even decided to move up the wedding date because he seemed so eager to make me his wife. I couldn't wait to have all of the people I love in our presence, sharing in our happiness and reassuring me that things would go smoothly when we actually say "I do".

———

Finally the big day has come! After a long four day work trip, I was anxious to get home to start preparing for our big dinner. Flying down I-395 in the sleek, new Audi that Jay recently purchased for me, I get a call from Josey so I answer immediately on the Bluetooth connection in the car.

"Hey Josey, are you excited for dinner tonight?"

Sounding completely out of it she responds, "Oh, Dee! Bad news!"

"Oh, no! Don't tell me you're not gonna make it either!"

"I hate to do this, but I feel like a whale over here and this baby refuses to come out! I'm just not sure I'll have the energy. And you know I hate driving that far into Virginia, especially with the baby being due at any moment."

"Oh, okay. I understand. The last thing I need is your water breaking in the middle of dinner!" I chuckle.

"Exactly! We don't need that! I'm sure we'll all be reunited at the hospital soon anyway once baby Troy decides to make his debut."

"I'm looking forward to meeting the little guy!"

"Me too! I'm just not looking forward to the labor pains."

"Ugh, I know! But I'll be there to hold your hand every step of the way!"

"Thank you, Dee. I wouldn't want anyone else by my side in that moment."

"Anytime, Toots."

"Are your parents still coming to your dinner?"

"My dad is, but my mom is on a cruise with her new boyfriend!"

"Yes! Get it Mama Davenport!" Josey says, giggling.

"I'm just happy that she has something else to focus on besides my love life these days!"

"Me too! Well send everybody my love. I know you have a lot of prepping to do for dinner tonight, so I'll let you go. But just remember to go light on the salt this time! You know how heavy handed you can be with it!" she warns.

"I'm sticking to the recipe this time! I promise not to go rouge again!" laughing in sync just as my father beeps in.

"My dad's calling on the other line, so we'll talk soon! Call me if you need anything!"

"Okay," she responds as I click over to take my father's call.

"Hey Dad!" I answer.

"Hey there, baby girl! How was work?"

"Not too bad, just excited to get home and start getting everything ready for tonight. How are you feeling about meeting Jay?"

"Like this meeting should've happened before he asked for your hand in marriage, but me and him will discuss that a little later on."

"Oh, Lord!" I exclaim at my father's disappointment in Jay's actions. "Well, he'll get the opportunity to ask you properly tonight!"

"As long as you're happy...that's really my main concern, Dulsey."

"I am Dad. I really am," I assure him. "I know our journey to get to this point hasn't been ideal, but we made it and we're both happy and want to be with each other. All I really need is just your love and support at this point."

"Then you have it. But he's going to get an ear full about what's going to happen if he ever hurts you again!"

"I wouldn't have it any other way!" I smile to myself at how good it feels to have my father being so protective over me. "Oh, what time does your flight get in again?"

"I land around three o'clock."

"Okay, I'll have a car service pick you up and take you to your hotel from the airport. That way you'll have some down time before dinner at eight. I'll have the driver come back to pick you up at seven-thirty and bring you to our house. Sound good?"

"Yep. Can't wait to see you, sweetie!

"Me either!"

I arrive home an hour later after making a quick pit stop at the grocery store for a few last minute items. I see Jay's car parked in the garage as I pull in. I wasn't expecting him to be home from practice so early, but since he's home, I'm hoping he'll want to help out in the kitchen. It may be the blind leading the blind when it comes to cooking, but between the two of us, I figure we can pull it off.

I walk through the garage door leading into the side hallway of the house that opens up into the kitchen. Lugging all of my luggage and a couple of light grocery bags, I drop my purse and toss my keys onto the counter next to a pile of semi-opened mail. I place my phone on the charger before I sift through the mail, grinning as I see my name on a few envelopes with my new address printed underneath, just as the last piece of mail catches my eye. At the bottom of the pile is an empty envelope addressed to Jay from a DNA testing lab. Scrambling through the stack of mail again, I look to see if I overlooked the contents of that envelop. Nothing. Not one single shred of paper with the laboratory's name on it.

Standing there with my hands planted firmly on the kitchen counter, I rack my brain wondering what this could pertain to as per Jay, his ex had given birth and it was found not to be his child. I grab the empty envelope and head up the mahogany, swirling staircase to question Jay about it.

Just as I approach the double doors of the master bedroom, I overhear Jay having a telephone conversation. I stand in the doorway watching him with his back towards me, facing the window holding the house phone to his ear in one hand and grasping a piece of paper in the other. I enter the room as he leans over and braces himself against the wall with the paper slightly balled up in his hand, when I'm stopped cold in my tracks as I get close enough to hear his actual conversation.

"Yeah, Mom. I know. Well at least I don't have any doubts now and I know that I'm the father..." his voice lingers.

I was frozen in motion by his words. This was really happening.

There's no more possibly — it's all real now. I didn't know what I was feeling; if I was more distraught over the fact that he actually has a child or that he found yet another way to blatantly deceive me. I let out a sigh of disbelief. He peeks over his shoulder, realizing that I was in the room then quickly ends his conversation and frantically hangs up the phone.

"Hey...hey babe," uncertain and caught off guard, I could tell he was trying to figure out how much of his conversation I had overheard. "Uhhh, I wasn't expecting you home so soon. How long have you been standing here?"

"Long enough to know that you're officially a father," I pause for a moment. Placing my hand over my stomach as I start to feel sick, I mutter, "Congratulations."

"Baby," he says hanging his head low, "I'm so sorry! I don't know where to begin." He rests his hands on the back of his head with his fingers interlocked, staring up at the ceiling. "This whole situation is such a mess right now. Come here...please. Let me talk to you!"

Staring at him in complete shock at a loss for words, I stumble backwards and turn to run into the bathroom, slamming the door shut and locking it behind me. With a nauseous feeling consuming me, I rush to the bathroom just in time. I continued getting sick for several moments as my head draped over the toilet. My heart starts to race and tears begin to pour down my cheeks at the mere thought

232   TASHA RAY

of how foolish I felt for actually thinking I was finally getting my happily ever after.

Jay begins pounding on the door aggressively trying to convince me to come out. "Baby, please! We need to talk about this!" After nearly twenty minutes of non-stop pleading, he finally relents leaving me in peace. I lean my head against the wall, drowning in my own thoughts trying to decipher through my feelings for what felt like an eternity. How can I compete with a child? I went from being the only one, back to not being a priority in a matter of seconds.

Once I'm finally able to muster up the energy, I strip myself naked, stepping into the oversized shower that we had made love in so many times. The water comes raining down over my face, washing away my tears. If only it could wash away all of the memories we shared and the intense feelings that I developed for him as well. I press my back against the faintly blue tile lined shower wall, dropping down on bended knee. Crying uncontrollably, I fall over sprawling my legs out, completely numb. Closing my eyes trying to make the tears stop as all of the blissful moments we shared began to flash through my mind; especially all the ones that I had envisioned, like our wedding day that will never happen now. He gave our future away to another woman and didn't even have the decency to inform me.

I sat in the same spot on that shower floor completely oblivious to how much time had passed as my tears finally dried up and the water grew cold, trickling down my legs. I feel like all the life has been sucked out of my body and I was left feeling like I was physically incapable of enduring anymore pain. I push the glass door open with my foot and crawl out of the shower, pulling a towel down from the rack just above me. I slowly dry myself off from head to toe, and then wrap myself in the coffee colored, silk robe hanging on the back of the door. Hoping not to see Jay, I quietly crack open the bathroom door before completely opening it and ducking into the closet adjacent to the hallway to throw on some clothes. Scrounging through all of the overpriced designer clothes he had gifted me, I finally find a plain tee shirt and jeans to quickly put on.

Just as I turn to exit the closet, I'm startled by Jay who is silently standing in the doorway watching me as I pull the pair of jeans over my hips. He looks away for a moment, exhaling, "Can we talk about this, please?"

I cut my eyes, and then brush past him walking into the bedroom to gather a few of my belongings.

"Dulsey, I never meant for this to happen and I didn't want you to find out like this. I'm sorry!"

"Aren't you tired of doing things that you have to constantly apologize for? I'm so damn tired of hearing 'I'm sorry', so I would think you would be tired of saying it!" Shaking my head out of frustration at the entire situation, I continue to pack my things before walking downstairs shortly after to prepare to leave.

Jay follows me downstairs and sits calmly on the barstool next to the kitchen island for a few moments, watching me gather all of my bags.

"So this it? This is how you want to leave things?" he asks as he stands up to approach me.

Thinking to myself for a moment, I decide that maybe I should tie up all the loose ends this time so he is clear that there are no more chances this go round. I drop my bags and turn around to address him once and for all. "I know you probably think that I'm incredibly naive," my voice starts to tremble as the hurt I'm feeling resurfaces and the numbness starts to dissipate, "and maybe I was for constantly turning a blind eye and being in denial about the person you really are." Unable to look him in the eyes as I attempt to suppress my anger, I turn my back to him and turn my eyes towards the pile of bags now strewed across the kitchen floor before I continue. "There were so many red flags all along, but I believed in you and always gave you the benefit of the doubt hoping you were better than that." Feeling the anger starting to reappear, I turn to address him, "And now look at you! I don't have a clue who you are! You're not the person you portrayed yourself to be in the beginning! And this...this isn't the man I fell in love with," I yell out, gesturing towards him. "You're a manipulative liar who preys on women's vulnerability for your own personal gain, and for that, you'll forever be a coward in my book!"

He attempts to interject, "Dulsey, I..."

"No! I'm not done yet!" I exclaim, waving my finger in his face. "Do you know the crazy part about all of this? Even after all the hurt and embarrassment you've caused me, I still don't hate you...I don't like your ass one bit, but I don't hate you. Because of you, now I know how strong I am and that I don't deserve a man that continually sets me up to fail." Wiping a tear away before it hits my check, I breathe out slowly, "I truly hope that one day you get it. I won't be around to witness it, but I hope that day comes for your son's sake. Hopefully he grows up to be the man you never could be."

I turn away and collect all of my bags and head out to the garage after swiping my keys from the counter. "I'll have Taylor come by and get the rest of my things."

Unsatisfied with my decision to leave, he gets up and pins me against the wall, begging me to stay. "No, Dulsey! You can't leave me like this! I love you too much!" He rests his head against mine as all of my bags fall to the floor.

I push him away, shaking my head at how things have unfolded. "It's just hard to believe that the person capable of making me feel so loved and worthy, could be capable of all the lies, deceit, and hurt that you've caused," I say somberly. "You were so broken and I knew that, but I wanted to help you pick up the pieces of your life and make sense of it all. I wanted so badly to show you that I could be everything that you always spoke of; that genuine person to love you for you, the one to show you what it feels like to really love someone beyond words. I wanted to be enough for you, but I was so wrapped up in what you wanted me to be, that I forgot what I needed from you. You were caught up in your own personal drama, between all of the women and your career that you couldn't see that I was broken too. I needed you to be someone that I'm not sure you'll ever be, and I think it's time that I stop neglecting my own feelings and worry about me for a change." I stop for a moment, nervously laughing to myself at the mere thought that I'm having this conversation with this man yet again. "You know, I've learned through this whole mess that no matter how resilient love is, trust is fragile and sometimes it's simply too late to get it right." I gather my bags again for the last time. Standing at the garage door, I turn and stare him directly in the eyes, "Your chances have run out, Jay. I hope that if nothing else, this situation will teach you to be a better man and father for your new family."

"Dulsey! Dulsey! Come on, you can't just walk out on me! I don't want to be with her, I want you!" he continues to shout as his words fall on deaf ears.

Just as I open the door, I turn as he walks towards me.

"I do have one question," I state calmly.

"Yeah, anything!" he responds.

"What's the baby's name?"

He quickly looks down at his feet, briefly closing his eyes before responding, "Jay Waters...Junior."

"Junior, huh?"

This guy never ceases to amaze me, I think to myself.

"Yeah...but Dulsey..." he attempts to explain as I cut him off.

"Jay, let it go. I know I have," closing the door in his face.

As I load up my car, all I can think about is the fact that he'll go into his next relationship without understanding my pain and the cycle will only continue with the next woman. I suppose it's true what they say, hurt people hurt people...I guess they don't know what else to do.

CHAPTER 26

Not wanting to chance the wrong song coming on and taking me back on an emotional roller coaster, I turn the radio off and ride in silence all the way home. Mentally and emotionally drained, all I want to do is lay in my own bed and be with my thoughts. Today seems to be the clearest that my thoughts have been in months, and I'm sure my dad will delight in this moment now that my engagement to Jay is off. I guess in my case, father knows best.

As I scramble through my purse looking for my phone to check in with my father, I become infuriated with myself after realizing I left it on the charger at Jay's house. Nearly home, I keep driving in hopes that Taylor won't mind going over to collect my phone and the rest of my belongings for me. To my surprise, Taylor is there waiting for me as I pull up. I park in front of my house right behind her car. Just as I open my door to question her, her car door swings open and she frantically runs towards me.

"Oh my God, Dee! What took you so long to get home?"

"Taylor, I got into it with Jay and..." I attempt to explain before being cut off.

"I know, I called your phone and he told me you guys had an argument and you left your phone. But anyway, Josey is in labor! Get your ass in my car and let's go!" she yells out.

Running to her car, we both hop in and quickly pull off.

"How is she? How long has she been in labor?" I question.

"Not long, she's not fully dilated yet so we have a little time to get there, but she's doing great from what her mom says. She told me twenty minutes ago that if anything changes, she would give me a call."

"Okay, good! What a fucking day! It's amazing how quickly things can change."

Taylor looks over side eyeing me with an "I told you so" look painted all over her face. Luckily, she spares me the lecture that usually accompanies that expression.

"Oh, shit! My dad! Where's your cell phone? I need to call my dad and tell him there's been a change of plans."

"It's in my purse, by your feet."

After sifting through Taylor's unorganized purse, I finally reach her cell. I dial my father's number several times, but it continues to go to voicemail.

"I guess I'll try him a little later. He must still be on his flight," I say, thinking out loud to Taylor.

"Yeah, that's probably it. Is this the right turn for the labor and delivery?" Taylor asks, confused by the signs.

"Yep, we're here. Hurry up and park! I can't miss this!"

———

Four hours later little Troy finally arrives. Josey coddles him, gazing into his eyes, finally learning the meaning of unconditional love in that moment. We look on in amazement and happiness, sharing yet another moment that will bond us together even tighter.

Wrapped up in the emotions of the day, I forgot to check back in with my father. We were in such a rush to check on Josey, neither of us noticed that I had left the phone in her car. Taylor walks out to the car to get her phone as Josey hands the baby to me to hold for the first time.

"Josey, he's perfect!" I say, with his little fingers wrapped around my thumb.

"He is, isn't he? I finally got to design my perfect man!" she chuckles.

"Well, you did a damn good job!" Gia adds.

"Thanks for being here with me guys. It really means the world to me!"

"Of course, Josey. Where else would we be? You know we love you to pieces! And now we have another addition to the family," I say looking down at baby Troy.

"Now it's your turn! Have you and Jay talked about when you'll start trying for kids?" Josey asks, unaware of what went down earlier.

Nervously smiling, I look away trying to fight back the tears.

"Are you okay?" a concerned Gia asks rubbing my back as she notices me getting teary eyed.

"Oh, yeah. I'm okay." Taking a moment to myself to process things, I stare deeply into the innocent eyes of this small life in my hands. "Jay and I broke up today. It seems that he wanted to start a family a little sooner than I did."

"That bastard!" Josey angrily mutters.

"Turns out the baby was his all along and he purposely misled me and had me thinking that he had actually resolved the matter before I agreed to marry him. He's the true definition of a habitual liar who is concerned with no one's feelings but his own."

"I'm sorry, Dee!" Gia gently expresses, still rubbing my back.

"Well, now you have a new man in your life! And I'm raising this one, so he won't turn out to be one of these knuckleheads out here!" Josey says.

"Good, because we have enough of those running around these days," Gia adds.

"But enough about me. Have you contacted Garrett?" I ask.

"I asked my mother to call him when she called you guys before I went into labor, but he hasn't responded," Josey shrugs, sitting back in the hospital bed as if the reality of her own drama filled relationship had just hit her. "I don't know how I'm going to do this or what role Garrett will play in his life, but I refuse to fail Troy and have him turn out to be anything like the men that we've been involved with."

"We'll do this together. Just like Taylor with Elijah and Gia with Elle, it's gonna work out just fine," I reassure her.

"But what if it doesn't? What if he shows up and then just disappears? It happened to you, Dee! Why couldn't it happen to Troy? I don't want Garrett to come and go, in and out of Troy's life as he pleases. I want my son to have consistency in every aspect of his life."

"Funny thing is I resented Robert so much for depriving me of twenty years of guidance, advice, and just the presence of a positive male figure. But truth be told, what my father should've told me then still couldn't prepare me for the pain I feel now." Shaking my head and laughing to myself, "Who knew? I guess life is funny that way. But I was lucky enough to get a second chance and every moment spent with him, I value greatly." Gia hands me a tissue, as the emotions of the day that I've tried so hard to suppress start to resurface. "I'm sure Garrett will come around in due time, and when he does, just let him be there for Troy. Don't let your issues come in between that relationship. Coming from someone who knows firsthand, he needs the both of you."

"You're right, Dee. It's not going to be easy, but I can't just shut him out of being his father. That wouldn't be fair and I don't want my baby boy to resent me for it when he grows up. Hell, who knows, maybe this is the wakeup call Garrett needs. Maybe he'll grow up and start acting like a man!" Josey says, sounding hopeful.

I stand up, and hand the baby over to Gia to hold. Just as little Troy leaves my arms, Taylor comes bursting through the door out of breath with her cell phone in hand.

"Taylor! What's wrong?" I ask out of concern.

Catching her breath, "Dee...your mother is on the phone. It's important! But have a seat first!"

"Hand me the phone," I interject.

Snatching the phone back, "Please, sit down first."

Sighing heavily, I sit back down and take the phone out of Taylor's hand.

"Dulsey?"

"Hey Ma, what's..." I attempt to question.

"Baby! Baby! Oh my Lord!" my mother cries out.

"What's going on? Are you okay?"

With only cries coming from the other end, I try to encourage her to continue, "Breathe! Tell me what happened!"

She continues to cry heavily, unable to formulate a coherent sentence before an eerie sense of calm falls over her long enough to utter, "He's dead, Dulsey! He's really gone this time!"

"Who? Who's gone, Ma?"

Her response triggered the most intense burst of emotion I have ever felt. I dropped to my knees, sulking uncontrollably at the mere sound of his name, now echoing through my head. From celebrating a life to being drained of it — and just like that, he was gone.

To Be Continued...

33714466R00148

Made in the USA
Middletown, DE
24 July 2016